THE
INTERRUPTED
EDUCATION
OF HUEY B

THE
INTERRUPTED
EDUCATION
OF HUEY B

NANCY J. HOPPER

LODESTAR BOOKS

Dutton　New York

No character in this book is intended to represent any actual person; all the incidents of the story are entirely fictional in nature.

Library of Congress Cataloging-in-Publication Data

Hopper, Nancy J.
    The interrupted education of Huey B / by Nancy J. Hopper. — 1st ed.
        p.   cm.
    Summary: Huey, in danger of failing senior English because he is monitoring the herons at a reservoir instead of attending class, further complicates his life by simultaneously dating two girls.
    ISBN 0-525-67336-9
    [1. Schools—Fiction.   2. Herons—Fiction.   3. Wildlife conservation—Fiction.]   I. Title.
PZ7.H7792In   1991
[Fic]—dc20   90-21231
                                                         CIP
                                                          AC

Published in the United States by Lodestar Books, an affiliate of Dutton Children's Books, a division of Penguin Books USA Inc.

Published simultaneously in Canada by McClelland & Stewart, Toronto

Editor: Virginia Buckley   Designer: Stanley S. Drate
Printed in the U.S.A.   First Edition   10   9   8   7   6   5   4   3   2   1

to Jim
and to Bass Catcher

THE
INTERRUPTED
EDUCATION
OF HUEY B

1

---

*F*ailing senior English? Me? I'd never failed anything
in my life. But there it was, a big, fat F, glaring up at
me from a deficiency slip, complete with a note to con-
tact my guidance counselor. I stared resentfully at the
old man, sleeping peacefully on the high bed. It was all
his fault.

Unaware, he slept on. His nose jutted sharp and
rigid above sunken cheeks. His forehead blended into
a path of white hair across the top of his head, bordered by a fringe of gray and black above his ears.

The other bed in the room was empty. Except for
the sound of voices down the hall and a light, whistling
snore from Lou, there was silence. I shoved my deficiency slip into a jeans pocket, then closed my eyes and
let my mind drift back to the best part of the day.

"Cut play practice," I'd urged, confident that Molly
would refuse. "Please." I brushed a hand over the short
bristles of my hair, rested the hand on the wall over
her head, and looked down at her.

Although she's tall for a girl, only four inches
shorter than I am, Molly's built generous, with nice

1

curves and long legs. Her hair is a mass of shining blonde curls that tumble loosely to her shoulders. She has blue eyes and a wide smile.

I'd have kissed her right there in the hall outside the auditorium, but the thought of her father interfered. Mr. MacWilliams, who is our assistant principal, is the same height as Molly, but his legs are short and muscular. His jowly face is topped by a mix of short black and gray hair. As he prowls the halls in search of trouble, his small eyes dart about suspiciously. Rumor has it that he has the personality of a pit bull with a toothache.

"Catch you later," I told Molly. As of three o'clock that afternoon, I'd never met her father, and I was hoping to keep it that way.

Since my Toyota was in the shop getting its brakes relined, I'd arranged a ride with The Bear. He was waiting for me, asleep behind the wheel of his mother's Escort. The sound of the passenger door closing woke him.

The Bear shook his head, blinked several times, and yawned before turning the key in the ignition. "Want to go to the mall?" he asked.

"Yeah. I'm supposed to meet Megan at The Hive."

The Bear slowed to let a truck pass before merging onto the expressway. "What'll happen when Molly finds out you're meeting another girl?"

"Nothing. It's not as if we're actually going together."

"Says who?"

"Me. We're both free to date other people."

"Sure." The Bear sounded so depressed I gave him a friendly punch on the shoulder.

"What's the matter?" I asked.

"Except for Missy Heagel in the third grade, I've

never had a girl friend. I keep wondering if there's something wrong with me."

"No way. You just haven't run into the right female yet."

"My mom's already nagging at me about the prom. She wants to know who I'm taking."

"I'll fix you up with somebody."

"Not like Homecoming." The Bear pulled into a slot near Revco, set the parking brake, and stared morosely through the windshield. "All Angie did was flirt with other boys."

"You should have danced with her more."

"She's so little. I was afraid I might break her."

"Come on," I said lightly. "Don't sweat the small stuff."

"Angie's small, all right. I felt like a gorilla next to her."

"So I'll find you a date with somebody bigger for the prom."

"Better start looking early." The Bear shoved his hands into his jeans pockets as we crossed the lot to the mall entrance. Although big flakes of snow were falling, he wore his lightweight Ravens jacket hanging open over his red sweat shirt. "Pick out a girl who's built sturdy, like me."

I didn't even want to think about a girl built like The Bear, let alone see one. I made reassuring sounds as we entered The Hive, then paused near the cash register to scan the tables and booths. The place was so jammed with kids and women loaded down with packages that it took me a couple of minutes to locate Megan. She was sitting in the last booth at the back wall, which I figured was a good spot. Megan's a junior cosmetology student, and although there are over two thousand students at Harrison High, Bear's comments

3

had made me uneasy. I knew I shouldn't be seeing two girls at the same time, but I liked both of them a lot.

"Have you been here long?" I asked Megan when I reached the booth. The Bear slid onto the bench opposite her, but I remained standing.

"Ten minutes."

"I'll get our stuff at the counter," I offered. "What do you guys want?"

"A large Pepsi," said Megan.

"A double cheeseburger and a chocolate shake," said The Bear. "I'll pay you back Saturday."

The people behind the serving counter were busy too. The milkshakes and Pepsi came right away, but it took a while for the double cheeseburger. While I waited, I sipped my shake and watched Megan and The Bear.

They looked somewhat strange sitting opposite each other. Both had very dark hair, but Megan's was long and straight, and Bear's was short and curly. I couldn't see the color from where I was standing, but I knew they had a similar shade of dark brown eyes too—Megan's soft and velvety, The Bear's surprisingly gentle in his masculine face.

Other than matching eyes and hair, the two had absolutely nothing in common. Megan is very slender, with a narrow face. She has a confident, straightforward way about her, friendly but assertive.

The Bear, who tends to be shy, was sitting in his typical position when he was alone with a girl. His head was ducked to avoid her gaze, and his entire body slumped in a futile attempt to make himself seem smaller. He was pulling at an imaginary thread on the cuff of his sweat shirt.

When I returned to the booth with the food, he and Megan were talking, or at least exchanging sentences. Suddenly Bear's eyes opened wide with astonishment.

4

"I don't believe this." He looked up at me. "She's never heard of me."

"Megan, this is Bear Scarpitti," I said. "Bear, this is Megan Albert."

"I already told her that," said Bear. "I told her I was The Bear. Then she said she'd never heard of me."

"What did you do?" asked Megan. "Hold up a bank?"

"He was all-state defense in football two years in a row," I explained.

"And she never even heard of me." The Bear swung his head back and forth in amazement.

"Sorry," Megan apologized. "I don't know much about football."

"That's okay," he said. "I don't know anything at all about manicures."

I put an arm around Megan to give her a quick hug. "How's my favorite girl?" I asked.

"Fine. How's Huey?"

"Great."

The Bear bent over his cheeseburger, hiding the sour expression that had appeared on his face. Since he's never been comfortable with his status of football hero, I was surprised he'd mentioned it to Megan. For someone his size, he likes to keep a low profile, especially around girls. When he finished his cheeseburger, he turned sideways in his seat, putting his back against the wall. He appeared to be unaware of Megan and me, holding hands under the table.

By the time we left the mall, the snow had changed to stinging sleet. The Bear hunched his shoulders against it and ran, slipping and sliding, toward his car. Halfway there, I let go of Megan's hand to turn my collar up against the wind. I was about to grab her hand again when I heard someone yell, "Huey!"

5

The chill that ran down my spine was in no way the result of weather conditions.

"Meet you at the car," I told Megan. "I have to get an English assignment." Without waiting for an answer, I jogged back to the mall entrance.

Molly was standing near the doors. Although she was partially sheltered from the wind, her cheeks were red and the tip of her nose resembled Rudolph the Reindeer's. Both her hands were shoved deep into the pockets of her red jacket. She freed one to pull her hair back from her face.

"We finished play practice early," she told me, "so I came out here to pick up my mother from work. I spotted Bear's car in the parking lot, but there weren't any empty spaces near it."

"We're just leaving." I stepped back and forth from foot to foot, trying to keep warm.

"Can't you stay?"

"I promised to be home by five."

Molly let go of her hair, which immediately flew back around her face. "Who's the girl?"

"A friend of Bear's."

"Bear Scarpitti has a girlfriend?"

"Not exactly," I hedged. "She's a girl and his friend. That's all." I bounced up and down, practically dancing from the cold. "They're waiting for me," I told Molly. "I'll call you tonight."

Back in the Escort, Bear was talking about football and Megan was looking terminally bored. "That was lucky," I told them. "I missed English again and didn't get the assignment. Mrs. Burr expects everything to be made up by the next day."

"Miss Cory gives us three days to catch up if the absence is excused," said Bear.

"That's because Miss Cory cares about her students," I told him. "All Mrs. Burr cares about is periods and participles."

"She—" The Bear broke off when the Escort went into a long skid. The world flashed by outside the windows, as if it were moving and the car was standing still.

Megan gasped as the car came out of the skid and immediately fishtailed. Bear's grip on the steering wheel tightened, but he didn't panic. He slowly brought the car under control.

"Let me off first," I said. "Then you won't have to swing back this way after dropping Megan off."

The Bear didn't answer, but ten minutes later he turned onto my street. I got out of the car, ran up onto our porch, and looked back to see his red taillights disappear into the sleet, now changing to rain. I'd had a couple of close calls in the past few hours, but I figured my troubles were over. I was in a terrific mood as I entered the house.

Dad was standing by the fireplace, one elbow on the mantle, his index finger stroking his mustache. He did not look very happy.

"Is there something wrong?" I asked.

"This." Dad held out a paper, which I recognized as my grade sheet.

I took the paper and looked at my grades—a solid line of A's and B's, interrupted by an F in English.

"What happened?"

I shrugged. How could I explain that crazy old man, Lou Erhart? I didn't understand him myself. "I was late a couple of times," I said slowly, "and I missed first period entirely once or twice." One of the times I was late, I'd missed part of the nine-week test, but I didn't tell Dad that.

"Why wasn't I notified that you had a grade deficiency?"

7

"It only happened the last couple of weeks." I shrugged. "It's my problem."

Dad scowled. "Contrary to your opinion, your grades are my problem too," he said. "I don't know what your mother would have done, but it's clear some sort of discipline is necessary."

I sighed. When Mom married Joel and moved to Chicago early in my senior year, staying with Dad had seemed the perfect solution. I didn't even have to change houses. Since Dad's lease was up on his apartment, he'd rented the house from Mom and moved in with me. I thought the biggest change would be that I might not smell dinner cooking when I arrived home from school.

I'd been wrong. I eyed the man in front of the fireplace. We shared the same name, the same height, and the same shade of gray eyes. We'd seen each other every other weekend for ten years. I'd gone white-water rafting with him, and once we spent a week together camping in a tent in the Grand Tetons. For all of that, it seemed I didn't know him.

"Huey?"

"If it was my fault, Mom would have grounded me, but this wasn't my fault."

"Why not?"

"Mrs. Burr grades too hard. She gave me a D on my last paper because I had two run-on sentences." As I explained, resentment toward Mrs. Burr built inside me. "She said no college-prep senior should be writing run-ons."

"She's right."

"I wouldn't mind a few points off, but two whole grades? None of the other teachers does that. As long as we have an excuse, they don't care if we're late or miss class either, but Mrs. Burr always takes off for it."

"So your grade is Mrs. Burr's fault."

8

Sensing a trap, I said, "Not entirely."

"Then whose fault is it?"

"Well," I said cautiously, "I kind of like to think of it as nobody's fault."

"You mean it just happened?"

"Yeah, that and Mrs. Burr."

And old man Lou Erhart, I had added to myself. My mind drifted back to where I sat in his room in the nursing home. I'd been staring so long at a blue rose on his blanket that my eyeballs felt dry and scratchy. I blinked several times to moisten them, then glanced at the man on the bed.

Lou was awake and watching me. His light blue eyes were sharp and piercing, totally alive in his pale face.

"That worthless, no-good Harold Benton show up with his shotgun?" he demanded.

"No."

"Then tell me about my birds."

What was there to tell? They were birds. So what?

"Well?" said Lou.

"There are lots of the big blue jobs out there," I began.

"Great blue herons," Lou interrupted.

"Yeah. And there must be a lot of fish too," I added, "because I saw one bird catch twelve in a half hour."

At Lou's nod, I went on, describing how many birds there were and where most of them fished, how many people were out in boats—information like that. I felt like a babysitter telling a story to pacify a cranky kid.

As I spoke, Lou's eyelids slowly drifted shut again. Within minutes he was asleep. I tiptoed out of the room, thinking that I really didn't mind visiting Lou or telling him stories. What I minded was all the trouble the old man had caused me.

9

2

When I joined the S-Team in January, I thought I'd be helping people with real problems, like being a big brother to a deprived kid or maybe giving another student the emotional support needed to keep off drugs. At worst, I figured I'd have to give up a couple of free hours a week to drive senior citizens to doctors' or dentists' appointments.

When I was assigned an old guy in a nursing home, I was a bit disappointed, but I didn't expect trouble. I figured I'd take him candy and a newspaper one afternoon a week and that'd be it. There was no way I could have known I'd end up crawling out of bed at 5:00 A.M. every Monday, Wednesday, and Friday, that I'd drive thirty miles before daylight, then sit in the car freezing my butt off in the interests of some scraggly birds that fished in the reservoir. I also didn't know that joining the S-Team could cause me to fail English.

Next to meeting up with Lou Erhart, being assigned Mrs. Burr in English was the most disastrous event of my four years of high school. Every single thing I'd told Dad about her was true, and more. Mrs.

Burr acts as if the whole reason for the students' senior year is so they can be in her class in English, learning about great literature and how a split infinitive could ruin their entire life. Every September seniors stand in lines at the guidance office, trying to dream up ways to get switched out of Mrs. Burr's English class.

I could have told Lou to get himself another watch-dog, but I didn't. He'd let me know he had gone to considerable trouble arranging for a township cop to keep his eye on the birds Tuesday and Thursday mornings, and that I was the third person from the support team he'd tried for the other weekdays. Lou's daughter lives near the reservoir, but she drives a school bus in the mornings. The first person quit after three weeks; the second wrecked his wheels and had to de-volunteer. I was it.

Don't sweat the small stuff, I told myself when I thought of English. Live now. Then I stepped up the activity I found most enjoyable: pursuing Molly and Megan.

Since Megan has to baby-sit her little brother every Wednesday after school, I offered to drive her home the next afternoon and help watch little Herbie, whom I'd never met. After dismissal, I met Molly for a couple of minutes, then hurried out to the car.

Megan was leaning against the passenger's side of my yellow Toyota. She waved when she saw me, then continued talking to Bear, who always parks in the lot by the gym.

Although that afternoon wasn't much warmer than the day before, Bear wasn't wearing a jacket. This left his favorite piece of clothing, a black sweat shirt, in full view. On the front of the sweat shirt in red letters is BE MORE LIKE BEAR. On the back is a red 28, Bear's number in football. As I approached, I heard him say,

"See. This is my number." He turned to display his massive back to Megan.

"I noticed," said Megan.

"You did?"

"I thought 28 was your I.Q."

Bear blinked. Then he grinned. "You're teasing me," he said.

Megan shook her head, laughing. Her long dark hair fanned in the air, then settled smoothly to her shoulders. I stopped beside her, draped an arm around her waist, and buried my nose in her hair.

Most of the girls in cosmetology experiment with their hair. They cut it in weird styles and dye it different colors until it looks and smells like a chemistry experiment. Not Megan. Hers smelled as clean and fresh as the fur of a cat who has been out in the cold. "Ready to go?" I asked.

"What kept you?"

"Trouble getting my locker open." I threw a quick wink at The Bear over Megan's head.

Bear didn't notice because he was looking at Megan. "Catch you guys tomorrow," he told us, then trudged off toward the parking lot near the gym.

My first view of Megan's house was the kitchen. It had the cleanest floor and the biggest refrigerator I've ever seen. The floor was white with little cubes of green; the refrigerator was a side-by-side with each side almost as large as our entire refrigerator–freezer. Its exterior was made of a substance the texture of melted marshmallows. The marshmallow-like material was the same shade of green as the cubes on the tile floor.

I was inspecting the inside of the refrigerator when Megan's brother and a friend arrived. "Who's that?" demanded her brother.

"Huey Blendenbacher."

"Why's he snooping in our refrigerator?"

"Looking for a snack," Megan explained. "Does Matt have to go home or can he stay to play?"

"I can stay," said Matt.

By that time, I had closed the refrigerator door and was examining the two kids.

They were bigger than I'd expected, maybe third- or fourth-graders. Megan's brother had large dark eyes like hers, but his dark hair was cut even shorter than mine, so that his scalp showed through. He was dressed in a dark brown knit shirt and camouflage-print pants tucked into what looked like miniature army boots. His friend was skinny and pale with tiny blue eyes and a large mouth. He had one tooth missing in the front.

"Is he your boyfriend?" Herbie demanded in mega-decibels.

"I don't know." Megan crossed her arms, cocked her head to one side, and considered me thoughtfully. "Are you my boyfriend?" she asked.

"If I had a list," I told her, "you'd be right at the top."

"Is this a date?" asked Matt.

"I don't think so," said Megan. "A date is when a guy takes a girl to the movies or to the prom, which happens to be coming up in about a month."

As Megan said that, I took a huge bite of the apple I'd found in the fruit bin. I'd forgotten about the prom.

"He sure is tall," observed Matt, running his beady little blue eyes up and down me.

"Why don't you guys go play in Herbie's room," suggested Megan. "I'll pop some corn and bring it to you."

Grumbling under his breath, Herbie left the kitchen, followed by Matt. While Megan got out pop-corn, oil, and a heavy pan, I finished the apple and resumed my investigation of the refrigerator. It wasn't very well stocked. "Why such a big fridge?" I asked as I let the door drift shut.

"My stepfather bought it when my two older brothers still lived at home. Then Sam got married and Roger joined the army." Megan shook the pan as the corn began to pop. "My stepfather moved out last summer and Mom's on a diet. My dad keeps telling Mom I'm too thin, but she can't keep a lot of high-calorie foods around or she'll eat them."

"You're not too thin," I told her. "I like the way you look."

"That's good because I don't think I'll ever be much heavier." Megan wrinkled her pretty little nose, then made a face.

On the pretext of checking the popcorn, I moved closer to her.

"Guidance called me in for counseling before Christmas," she said, "because there was a rumor going around school that I'm anorexic."

"You're perfect." I put an arm around her, resting my hand on her hip. She felt firm and sleek, muscular rather than soft.

As Megan lifted the popcorn from the heat to a front burner, she glanced up at me. My lips touched hers—

"*Ack, ack, ack!*"

"*Diz! Diz!*" A camouflaged figure slid on its side across the kitchen floor. A second commando, dressed in black, leaped through the doorway, his green assault weapon at the ready.

"Hands on your head!" shouted the one on the floor, his rifle aimed at my face. Then he screamed, "It's an alien, infiltrating our line."

My plan for the afternoon with Megan fell apart. The low point came when I found myself crawling on my knees and elbows behind their pink living room couch, a plastic bayonet between my teeth. When I

14

stopped crawling, Herbie prodded me in the rear with his grenade launcher. "They're on the other side of this hill," he warned.

Megan and I weren't even in the same squad.

3

I was inspecting a carpet burn on my elbow the next morning when The Bear appeared at my locker. "What are you doing here this early?" I asked, since Bear usually arrives at school barely in time not to be marked tardy.

"I woke up and couldn't go back to sleep," he explained. "How'd you make out yesterday?"

"All right," I muttered, pulling my sleeve down over the carpet burn and buttoning the cuff.

"Score any touchdowns?"

"Touchdowns?" As I turned cynical eyes on him, I reminded myself that The Bear had been my best friend since middle school.

"You know." Bear shifted his books from his right hand to his left, then rubbed at his chin. He'd shaved badly that morning; there was a razor scrape among the black stubble left from his efforts.

I eyed the sparse, curling hairs growing on the back of the hand that rubbed his chin. More hair crept from the top opening of his striped oxford-cloth shirt. "Why

16

are you all dressed up?" I said. "Where's your sweat shirt?"

Bear didn't answer my questions. "So what happened?" he asked instead.

"Nothing."

Bear dropped his hand from his face and frowned as if he didn't quite believe me.

"I'd just started to kiss her when her kid brother and his little friend decided to play Rambo," I explained. "I spent the next two hours crawling around on my hands and knees, picking up carpet burns and pretending I was the enemy."

When Bear laughed, I added, "It's not funny. This has been the most rotten week I've ever lived through. Today's not going to be any better either."

"Why not?"

"I have to report to guidance first period to discuss my English grade. The only good part of that is I don't have to face Mrs. Burr today."

Although Bear made a sympathetic sound, there was no way he could understand what it's like in Mrs. Burr's class. His English teacher, Miss Cory, is young and pretty, and she understands when people can't find time to study. Mrs. Burr is middle-aged and looks like Benjamin Franklin. She thinks her class is the most important event ever to take place at Harrison High.

"Mrs. Burr didn't give me a fair chance to make up the work I missed," I told Miss Panasek, my guidance counselor, that afternoon.

"So Mrs. Burr is responsible for your bad grade?"

"Not entirely." I tried to cross my legs but couldn't. A bookcase touched the back of my chair; Miss Panasek's desk crowded me from the front.

"Mrs. Burr is one of our most caring teachers," Miss

17

Panasek told me. "There's not a person in the school system who works harder than she does."

When I think of a caring person, I think of someone like Grandmother Blendenbacher, not Mrs. Burr. I stifled a sigh.

"According to the report Mrs. Burr filled out, you had a C the end of last semester," continued Miss Panasek, studying the comment sheet in front of her. She twisted a short brown curl around one finger, then dropped the curl to shift the paper, bringing the print into better range for her bifocal lenses. "What happened?"

"I don't know."

"There must be a reason. Did something change in your life since then? Was there a family illness or a problem between you and your parents?"

"I joined the S-Team," I said, "and the old guy I'm assigned is in a nursing home. He has the idea somebody's going to wipe out his birds while he's in there."

Miss Panasek looked blank.

"The birds are great blue herons. They eat a lot of fish out of the reservoir," I told her. "Some man who fishes there shoots at them."

"What does this have to do with your English grade?"

"The old guy's daughter lives in a house overlooking the reservoir," I explained. "She keeps an eye on the herons, but she drives a school bus mornings. Someone has to watch the birds from six to eight; I'm it Mondays, Wednesdays, and Fridays." I tried to cross my legs again and failed. As well as being very small, Miss Panasek's office was much too hot. There were patches of sweat on my back, causing my shirt to stick to my skin.

"Three tardies make an absence," I added, "and Mrs. Burr doesn't care whether it's excused or not." My anger at Mrs. Burr returned, making my voice sound bitter. My grade *was* Mrs. Burr's fault. She could have given me a break. "Some teachers don't even check attendance," I pointed out.

"What about this past week? Have you been late or missed any of her classes?"

I stared at Miss Panasek. Although she isn't stupid, at the moment she seemed like it.

"Monday I fell asleep watching the birds and then had to wait for a stupid train at the railroad crossing. I made it to class before the passing buzzer to second period, but Mrs. Burr marked me absent anyway." I cleared my throat. "Tuesday and yesterday were no problem."

"Today?"

"This is first period."

Miss Panasek's cheeks reddened, but she only said, "And tomorrow?"

"I'll make it tomorrow," I promised, although the next day was Friday. I could cut fifteen minutes off my two-hour watch, although that would leave the herons unprotected during that time. It was no big deal. I'd been going out to the reservoir for almost a month, and the only other person I'd ever seen there was the township cop.

"And you will catch up with the rest of the class?"

"I'm not behind," I told her. "I always make up the work."

"So the problem really is tardiness and absences."

"Yes." I leaned back in the chair. Then I had an absolutely brilliant idea, so brilliant I could hardly believe I thought of it. "If I had a different teacher," I said, carefully laying groundwork, "one who didn't care so much about kids missing class . . ."

"You must realize it's against school policy to transfer a student from a teacher he's been assigned."

"But this is a special case," I protested. "I have a real problem with Mrs. Burr. I don't much like her and she hates me."

"I'm certain Mrs. Burr doesn't hate you," said Miss Panasek. "You could misunderstand each other or have a conflict of personalities."

"That's it," I said. "We have a personality conflict."

Miss Panasek thought for a while. Then she said, "We try to balance our teachers' student loads, especially in language arts."

"Sue Evans had Miss Cory first period, and Sue moved last month, so there's room in that class," I pointed out.

Miss Panasek frowned.

I held my breath.

"Well . . ."

"I know Mrs. Burr would be glad to get rid of me," I added. "I sit in the front row near her desk, so every single time she looks up, there I am—not that I ever cause trouble."

When my eyes met Miss Panasek's, I assumed a warm, innocent expression. "It would mean a lot to me," I said in a low voice.

Miss Panasek glanced at the comment form, then opened her top desk drawer and shuffled through its contents. She took out a small pad of pink slips and wrote rapidly across one. "I shouldn't do this," she told me, "but if it will solve your problem—"

"Thanks." I grabbed the pink slip before she could change her mind.

"Have Miss Cory sign on the top line and Mrs. Burr sign on the second. As soon as the form's returned to me, you can switch classes."

"Terrific," I said. "Great." I got up and backed toward Miss Panasek's office door, trying to keep the joy that exploded inside me from showing on my face. "I'll get the form back to you as soon as possible."

When she handed me a pass to class, the secretary in the outer office observed, "You certainly are cheerful today. Did you win the lottery?"

"Hey," I said, waving the precious pink slip at her, "I just won something *better* than the lottery."

4

I don't know if it was because the herons were my passport out of Mrs. Burr's class, but suddenly they appeared a lot more attractive to me. In the weeks I'd been guarding them, those birds had reminded me of prehistoric flying creatures, put together from left-over bird parts. Their toes were long and fingerlike, their yellowish legs like stilts. An enormous yellow and black bill served as a lethal weapon to catch and kill fish.

Even the name *great blue heron* didn't make sense, since their bodies and huge wings were more gray than blue. The forward view of one standing, black-and-white-striped belly touching water and head tilted to one side, resembled an oversized feathered golf club.

Although it was only the last week in March, already the days were lengthening. I had arrived at the reservoir before full daylight, driven down the lane, and parked in my usual spot, near the water on a spit of hardened earth fishermen used as a boat ramp. I ran the wipers to clear the windshield of moisture, then killed the engine and rolled down the window next to me.

As I sat watching, patches of light enlarged until the entire sky was blue. I could see the small island near the center of the water and beyond that the house on the hill where Lou's daughter lived. PUBLIC FISHING AREA proclaimed the sign three feet from my bumper. NO MOTORS.

By full daylight the first of the herons had arrived, its long neck curled into a loop, five-foot wings held out with their primaries fanned for brakes. The bird extended its landing gear and settled gently into shallow water. It shook itself, lifting the white feathers on its forehead into a sort of crest. The feathers on its skinny neck stood erect, and its body looked twice its actual size. As the feathers settled, the heron peered intently at my yellow Toyota, then gave the croak I'd come to recognize as a signal of displeasure. It waded off, head cocked in search of breakfast.

By the time I left the parking area, there were several dozen herons fishing. Some were on the far side of the reservoir, too far for me to do more than identify them as the same species as those who fished the water by the island or along the shore closer to my car. There were loads of herons, but no sign of Lou's arch enemy, the hated Harold Benton. I was beginning to wonder if Lou had made the man up.

By cutting fifteen minutes off my guard duty, I made it to school well before the late buzzer. I stopped by my locker, then headed for Miss Cory's room on the third floor.

Miss Cory was absent. Deciding one more period with Mrs. Burr wouldn't kill me, I went to her class on the second floor.

"On time for a change, Huey," she said.

I smiled and mumbled something, then sat at my desk in the front row.

If Mrs. Burr was aware her chances to educate me would soon be terminated, she gave no outward sign. She proceeded with the scheduled review for the first big test of the grading period, due to take place Monday.

While other students lapped up every hint she dropped about the test, I lounged in my seat thinking kind thoughts about Miss Panasek and Miss Cory. Monday morning I'd get Miss Cory's signature. Then I'd present the pink slip to Mrs. Burr. I'd never even have to write my name on the stupid test paper. I yawned widely. I was going to love Miss Cory's class.

"Are we boring you, Mr. Blendenbacher?" asked Mrs. Burr, who is the only teacher who ever uses my full last name.

"On, no," I said cheerfully.

"Do you have any questions?"

I pretended to think for a second, then shook my head.

"Then I'll expect an A on your test." After glaring at me over the top of her wire-rimmed half glasses, she looked at the other students. "Following Monday's test on grammar and punctuation," she told them, "we will use the remaining weeks of the grading period to complete work on your research paper and to study *Macbeth*."

I smiled in utter contentment. I'd have to write the research paper because all senior college-prep students had to, but Miss Cory would be grading mine. At the sound of the passing buzzer, I gathered my books. I'd just spent my last hour ever in Mrs. Burr's room.

"Lucky dog," muttered Adam as he passed me on the way out of the room. I glanced at Mrs. Burr to see if she'd heard, but she was busily arranging papers on her desk.

If Mrs. Burr was unaware of my precious pink slip, then she was one of the few people at Harrison High who didn't know about it. On the way into pre-calculus, I was practically mobbed.

"Show it to me again," demanded JoJo Jones, who, along with Molly and Randall—a black friend of mine—has Mrs. Burr seventh period. "I think it's fake."

Since I knew JoJo's mother had sent a written request that JoJo be put in a different class from Mrs. Burr's, I tolerated his accusation. I merely pulled out my wallet, removed the pink slip, and held it up for everyone to admire.

"I don't believe this," said JoJo. "You got yourself pink-slipped when my mom failed me."

"Can I hold it a minute?" asked Alice Anderson, who doesn't have Mrs. Burr for English but is aware of her reputation as a teacher.

"Sorry," I told Alice. "This stays in my possession."

JoJo cocked his head at me, his black eyes resentful. "I think you stole the slip and forged Miss Panasek's signature," he said.

I looked superior.

Randall, who's been in most of my classes since the second grade, was watching all this from his position leaning against the chalkboard. As he shrugged away from the board, his eyes met mine over the heads of the shorter students. He shook his head and gave me his laid-back smile. "Man," he said, "I thought this was something even you couldn't do."

"Never underestimate my powers of persuasion," I said.

"You have something on Miss Panasek?"

"She was overwhelmed by my irresistible charm."

"Tell you what," said Randall. "I'll give you ten dollars for that slip."

The late buzzer sounded. Mr. Eldrich was in the room, but he didn't interrupt us.

"Sorry," I said, "but this pink slip can't be transferred. My name is on it."

"I'll give you ten dollars anyway. I like the idea of owning something no one else in the whole world has."

"It isn't for sale."

At this point Mr. Eldrich decided to hold class.

"Eat your hearts out," I told the other kids as I went to my desk. "I'll be in Miss Cory's class, relaxed and happy, while you're working away on that research paper and memorizing long speeches from *Macbeth*."

"Tell us how you did it," whined JoJo.

"I'll think about it," I promised, "over the weekend while you guys are studying for the test."

5

―――――

I tacked the pink slip to the bulletin board over my desk at home, where I could see it every time I entered my bedroom. I already had Miss Panasek's signature, and Miss Cory's was a sure thing. After securing both signatures, I'd appear in English Monday as if showing up for class. While the rest of the students watched, I'd present my pink slip to Mrs. Burr and be free from her clutches forever.

Meanwhile, I intended to enjoy my weekend date with Molly. Although Megan was visiting her father, I decided there was no reason to risk one of her friends seeing me at the Youth Center dance with another girl. Saturday night I headed north on the expressway instead of turning south in the direction of the Youth Center.

"Where are we going?" asked Molly.

"I'm bored with the Youth Center," I said. "Let's do something different."

"Like what?"

"Like roller skating."

"Roller skating?" Molly repeated as if she'd never heard of it.

"I thought of taking you mud wrestling, but I figured you wouldn't want to mess up your clothes."

"But we don't have skates."

"We can rent them."

When Molly didn't answer, I added, "If you really want to go to the dance, we can."

"Skating might be fun. I haven't tried it since I was a Brownie Scout."

"Is that good or bad?"

"We'll find out."

The parking lot at Night Sky Rink consisted of gravel interspersed with mud. There was a lone security light, which flickered spastically as if it were going to flake out any minute. The gravel crunched under our feet as we crossed the lot.

Two biker types stood on the narrow cement slab in front of the entrance, blocking the door. One was fairly tall, wore his black hair in a thick pigtail, and had a small gold ring in his left nostril. The other was very short and wide. They both wore leather jackets, jeans, black boots, and wallets attached to chains heavy enough to be used as weapons.

Since neither showed any sign of moving, I said, very politely, "Excuse me."

The short biker looked at me. "How's the weather up there?" he asked. The biker with the pigtail and nose ring was staring at Molly. Fortunately, Molly was looking at the short biker and didn't notice.

"Cold." I shivered. "Can we go inside?"

"Feel free." He stepped off the cement to let us pass.

About ten feet inside the entrance was a combination ticket counter and coatroom. Behind the counter, in addition to the gray-haired woman in charge, was a long rack with numbered hangers. Above the rack were three signs. One said NO SPITTING. The second warned: NO TICKET—NO COAT; and the third was in favor of proper dress at all times.

Although the building wasn't much warmer than the parking lot, Molly didn't seem to mind. She peeled off her jacket, then dug through the pockets to remove two small combs before giving it to the woman. While I paid, Molly used the combs to fasten her long hair away from her face. "I want to see where I'm going," she explained.

The man at the rental counter came up with skates to fit me right away, but he had to hunt for a pair Molly's size. While we waited, Molly watched the skaters circling the smooth, rectangular floor. The eager expression on her face indicated she thought skating was a good idea. I hoped so. The more I was with Molly, the better I liked her.

When the rental man finally found skates to fit Molly, she and I circled the rink to a bench where we could sit to put them on. Near the bench was a long brass rail, which separated the rink from the sitting area. The brass shone like gold, polished by thousands of hands passing over it.

I'd forgotten how noisy roller rinks are. Although the background music was probably at full volume, it only came through in bursts. The dominant sound was the singing of hundreds of wheels, interspersed with shrieks from mobs of children, who ducked in and out of other skaters, zipping along like mini speed demons.

The first five minutes after putting on my skates, I stood hanging on to the brass rail and feeling like a fool. Molly spent almost the same amount of time hanging on to me. She'd let go for a couple of seconds, then grab me again as the skates beneath her headed off in different directions.

Molly gained control over her wheels first. She

29

made short expeditions away from me, then turned to come back again. She looked even better on skates than in regular shoes. The skates made her legs look very long in their smooth, tight jeans.

I'd just started making forays onto the floor when the skate-rental man, who also served as a DJ, announced, "Here's an easy one for beginners. Experienced skaters, make way for the learners." That cleared most of the adults off the floor, along with a lot of the mini speed demons. With Molly's encouragement, I managed to skate twice around the rink without falling.

"And now couples," said the DJ. "We will have couples only, ladies and gentlemen."

I took refuge at the rail, hanging my elbows over it to keep myself upright.

Evidently *couples* meant anybody who was willing to skate two by two. Knots of little girls went by holding hands; there was an occasional male with a female and some adults with children in tow. The DJ dimmed the white lights and lit flickering blue ones. "Get with it, fellows," he urged. "Take you favorite lady for a spin around the floor."

"Come on, Huey." Molly tugged at me.

The tall biker went past, skating slowly. In front of him, held securely upright by his hands, was a small girl dressed in green pants, a Mickey Mouse sweat shirt, and a pair of tiny white shoe skates. She attempted to skate to the music, her tongue sticking out between her teeth as she concentrated.

"Will the tall gentleman with the pretty blonde lady take her onto the floor," said the DJ.

"He means us," Molly told me.

I pried myself from the rail, managed to make about six feet without falling, then retreated to safety. "The music's too fast," I said.

"We have an amateur here," announced the DJ, "just dying to get in on the fun. Give the man space, friends, lots of space."

I wanted to crawl under the rail and hide beneath a bench. Instead, I gritted my teeth and tried again.

"Glide," Molly advised.

"I think there's something wrong with my skates."

"Come on, silly," she said. "You can do it."

"One more turn with your sweetheart, folks," said the DJ. "We have skaters just busting to roll. Can't keep them waiting on the sidelines."

I was beginning to realize I could not only stay upright, but maybe could even enjoy skating, when the music picked up volume and speed. The blue lights went off, and the white lights brightened. "All right!" screamed the DJ. "Everybody roll!"

Three kids the size of Megan's brother appeared from nowhere. They shot past us like guided missles, low and deadly. Behind them, skating at a more leisurely pace, his hands behind his back and his chunky body somehow graceful, was the short biker. The chain to his wallet glowed silver in the bright lights. The stones in the rings he wore glinted red and blue.

Five feet in front of us, the short biker made a sudden shift in his forward movement. Then he was skating backward, grinning at us. When I muttered "Show-off," his grin widened and he gave me a thumbs up. Seconds later, he turned and disappeared into the other skaters.

On the far side of the rink, a skinny man in a cowboy shirt and black jeans had corralled the three guided missiles. He herded them under a sign that advised: IF IT ISN'T YOUR BUSINESS, DON'T ASK QUESTIONS. As Molly and I passed, I heard him threaten, "Once more and you're outta here."

I suffered a few lumps and bruises, but by the end

of the evening, I had my skates under control most of the time. At that point Molly had mastered hers, moving in long, smooth glides around the floor, one hand clasped in mine. There was no doubt she was enjoying herself. She told me later, when I parked in front of her house shortly after twelve.

"Are you sure you didn't get hurt when we fell?" I asked.

"Which time?" Molly brushed my cheek lightly with warm fingers. "Thanks, Huey," she said. "I had a terrific evening."

I leaned over the parking brake to kiss her. Her lips tasted faintly of the pizza she'd eaten. I kissed her again, then said, "Let's move to the backseat."

"Why don't we go in the house?" said Molly.

"Won't your parents be up?"

"They go to bed after the eleven o'clock news." Molly unlatched the passenger door. "Besides, my dad doesn't like me to sit out front in a car with a boy. He says it doesn't look nice."

Anything to please Mr. MacWilliams. Feeling as if I were entering the lair of a dangerous animal, I followed Molly up onto the porch and into the house.

There wasn't a thumbscrew or a cattle prod in sight. The living room was decorated in what's called early American, with long, white ruffled curtains and wallpaper covered by stripes and little pink flowers. A miniature blackface sheep stood guard beside the fireplace. The chair next to the sheep was upholstered in pale pink. Matching pillows were arranged on a flowered couch, which looked as if it were stuffed with down. I sank into the couch.

I was going to suggest that Molly join me when upstairs a toilet flushed. I sat bolt upright—as upright as a person can when he's wallowing in down.

"You said your parents go to bed right after the news!"

"That doesn't mean they're asleep." Molly held out a hand to me. "Come on. Let's raid the refrigerator. Mom made an apple pie."

Food's always been a comfort to me, especially when I'm nervous, and I definitely was nervous. The very thought of her father on the prowl was enough to launch me out of the sofa and on my way to the kitchen. If Mr. MacWilliams did decide to come down-stairs, I'd look a lot more innocent eating apple pie than kissing his daughter.

"How is it?" Molly asked when she'd served me a large slice of pie. She sat beside me at the table, resting her head on the palm of one hand. Her long blonde hair made a curtain between me and the doorway to the living room.

"Best pie I ever tasted. Aren't you going to have any?"

"I have to watch my weight."

"No, you don't."

"I need to lose at least ten pounds."

"No way," I protested. "You have a perfect shape."

"Really?" Molly looked doubtful. "I think I'm fat."

"Forget that," I told her. "Hugging a skinny girl is like wrapping your arms around a bundle of sticks."

"You're sweet."

The expression in Molly's eyes was so inviting that I almost suggested we go back to the living room couch. The sound of something like a chair scraping the floor upstairs changed my mind. After the scraping noise, very distinctly, someone belched. "You have any more pie?" I asked.

I watched gloomily as Molly cut me a second slice. Since I'd eaten most of the pizza, I was already stuffed, but I didn't want to go home, and I sure didn't want to be cuddled up with Molly on the couch if her father appeared.

It wasn't as if I'd done anything to feel guilty about, I told myself as I began eating the pie. I was perfectly innocent. No one could punish me because of the private thoughts that went through my head and passed around my body until they settled in appropriate places. I concentrated on the white ceramic goose in the center of the kitchen table and tried to forget about Mr. MacWilliams. The goose had a blue ribbon with tiny white flowers tied in a bow on its neck. The top edge of the beak had been chipped. Someone had repainted it with the wrong shade of yellow.

I know it's not possible, but I felt as if Molly's father had X-ray vision, as if he could look right through the floor at Molly and me. Personally, I didn't need X-ray vision. I could see Mr. MacWilliams all too well in my mind: his thick, coarse skin drooping into jowls along the line of his jaw and his fierce eyes smoldering under his single black eyebrow.

I ate three pieces of pie, a glazed doughnut, and an apple. Every time I'd stop eating, I'd hear some little sound coming from upstairs—a grunt, a groan, and once the sound of footsteps. The footsteps went out of the room overhead, down the hall, and stopped at what I guessed was the top of the stairs.

There were no footsteps returning to the room overhead.

There was no more apple pie either.

"Want some leftover macaroni and cheese?" asked Molly.

"No, thank you." Like the nice boy my mother always taught me to be, I politely thanked Molly, gave her a quick good-night kiss, and fled to the safety of my car.

6

When I called her house Sunday, Megan answered the phone. "I didn't stay over at Dad's," she explained. "We only went out for dinner and a video. He dropped me off at the Youth Center about ten."

"See anybody I know?"

"Your friend, The Bear."

"Who was he with?" Bear hadn't told me he was going to the dance.

"Some other football players. I asked him to dance."

"Did he step on your feet?"

"He didn't get close enough." Megan laughed. "He *was* pretty nervous," she told me, then asked, "What are you doing this afternoon?"

"Visiting Lou at the nursing home. Want to come along?"

"Sure." Megan agreed right away, which surprised me, since I thought she'd probably be put off by going anywhere near a nursing home.

"This place isn't too bad," I assured her later that afternoon when we arrived at Middlebury Manor. "Especially this wing." I pulled open one of the large double doors, and we went inside. "A lot of the patients have hardly anything wrong with them."

"I know that," said Megan. "I used to visit when my stepmother worked here." She bent over, slapped at one leg, and whistled softly. "Here, Ace," she called.

Ace, the shaggy little black dog who'd stuck his head from behind the nurses' station, dashed in our direction. He sat up on his bottom, resting one paw on Megan's knee.

"Good boy." Megan pulled a treat from her jacket pocket and gave it to him.

"That dog should be on a diet," a passing nurse told us. "He's way overweight."

Evidently Ace didn't understand what she'd said because he followed the nurse, his tongue hanging out and his tail wagging. When she turned off at the nurses' station, he trotted on down the hall, passed several open doors, and disappeared into the recreation room.

"Ace always ignores me," I complained.

"Bring him a piece of trail bologna," Megan advised. "He'll be your friend for life."

Like most of the other doors on the hall, the door to Lou's room stood open. When Megan stopped to talk with a lady in a wheelchair, I breezed in.

Lou had acquired a roommate since I'd last visited him. The roommate was a middle-aged man with both legs and one arm in a cast. He was reading a magazine but glanced up as I entered the room.

"Been wondering where you were," said Lou.

"I stopped to pick up my girl friend. How are you doing today?"

"No problem." Lou waved an impatient hand. Although he was lying on his bed, he was dressed in a plaid shirt and dark brown pants. "You see Bass Catcher yet?"

"Not yet." Bass Catcher was Lou's special bird. Lou claimed that the bird had shown up every spring for the past twelve years, that he could be identified by the single black plume that grew in the white feathers of his forehead.

"Probably dead in a ditch somewhere."

"Not necessarily," I said. "I can't see the herons on the far side of the island well enough to identify individuals."

"That excuse won't work after today," said Lou. "I'm going to lend you my field glasses." He pointed at his dresser. "Top drawer."

Lou's binoculars looked expensive. As I returned them to their heavy leather case, I told him, "I can't borrow these. What if I lose them?"

"You won't. There's a present for you too, under the binoculars."

Lou's present was a field guide to birds east of the Rocky Mountains. I was leafing through it when Megan came into the room.

When I'd introduced them, Lou observed, "Fella here can't tell a Canada goose from a mallard."

"I can too!"

"Doesn't like being teased either." Lou winked at Megan. "I can't see why a pretty girl like you would hang around a fella like that."

"No accounting for taste," Megan responded cheerfully.

"He ever take you out to see my birds?" asked Lou.

When Megan said "All I get is promises," I stifled a groan. I knew exactly what was going to happen to the remainder of the afternoon. Fifteen minutes later, the two of us were headed for the reservoir.

"It's getting so I could drive this road in my sleep,"

I complained as I pulled onto the long lane leading to the parking area. "Lou asked for somebody from the S-Team who was interested in biology. It doesn't make the slightest difference to him that I'm interested in microbiology."

"This is a super place," said Megan, ignoring my complaints. She rolled down her window to let in a rush of cold, damp air, filled with the scent of wet leaves, pine, and mushrooms. A small branch brushed her side of the Toyota, causing her to jerk back from the window. "Have you seen any deer out here?"

"The second morning. I was sitting in the car when three of them came out of the trees on the island. They walked almost belly deep into the water to drink."

"I wonder how they got to the island."

"Probably swam." I pulled into a parking slot facing the water and killed the engine.

Although there were two other cars in the area and a new blue pickup truck with temporary tags, there were no people nearby. I looked across the reservoir toward Lou's daughter's house. A couple of kids played near the water's edge. Behind them, a woman sitting in a lawn chair put a hand to her head.

I focused on the kids, then on the woman, with Lou's binoculars. They had good-quality lenses. With a few minor adjustments to suit my eyes, I could see perfectly.

The woman was staring back at me through her binoculars. She waved.

I waved back. "I think I just met Lou's daughter," I told Megan.

"Where are all the herons?"

"They'll be around. They do most of their fishing in the early morning or late afternoon, except for when they have chicks. Lou says the parents have to fish all day then."

When Megan didn't answer, I added, "Herons can be shy around people too. Lou told me they seem to accept fishermen, but they don't like other people, especially those carrying guns and cameras."

"Oh, Huey! Look!" Megan pointed.

About fifteen feet out in the water, a small bird had surfaced. It seemed to tread water, staring at us, then doubled over and disappeared beneath the water again. Seconds later it came up in a place several yards from where it had submerged. Just when I'd located it in the binoculars, it disappeared again.

After three more tries, I finally managed to zero in on the creature. It had a roundish head, dark eyes, and a black ring around a thick, gray beak.

"Huey!" Megan grabbed my arm, shaking it. "What's that?"

A very large great blue heron had landed partway out toward the island. It lifted its feathers and shook them, looked intently at our car and us for several seconds, then stared into the water. The bird moved into a patch of dead cattails and out the other side, striding at a slow, majestic pace.

"Its knees work backward from ours," said Megan in a low voice.

"Those are ankles," I whispered back. The heron was what Lou called an "A" bird. Maybe it was the light—sun filtering through a slightly overcast sky—but the heron looked very blue across its back and wings. The white of its forehead was crisp, and it possessed a long fall of pale grayish plumes across its back and down its front—long enough for the front plumes to touch water as it waded, its neck in a curve over the surface of the reservoir.

Through the binoculars, the strong, resilient muscles of the bird's neck were clearly defined under a soft cover of gray feathers. The front of the neck, striped

39

black and white like the bird's stomach, was immaculate. Long black plumes extended from the back of the black patches bordering its white forehead. An additional black plume rose directly from the forehead itself, curving backward over the crest of the head.

While I watched, the heron struck, lifted its head, shook it, hesitated, and struck again.

The second time the heron's head rose above the water, there was a huge fish impaled on its beak. Although the heron held its prey as high as it could, the tail of the fish dragged in the water. From the tense curve of the bird's neck, I knew the fish had to be very heavy.

Megan had been tugging at my arm, asking me a question.

"Bass Catcher," I answered her.

7

Of course, I didn't study for the test Sunday evening.
After I dropped Megan off at her house, I went to Middlebury Manor to tell Lou that Bass Catcher was back
at work at the reservoir. Then I went home, loaded up
on dinner, and spent the evening watching the movie
channel.

People didn't get much luckier than I was: president of the Key Club with two girl friends so terrific I
couldn't even choose between them, and now the possessor of a magic pink paper that would free me forever
from the clutches of Mrs. Burr. Early Monday morning
I cut out on Bass Catcher and the other birds and arrived at school in time to get Miss Cory's signature before the tardy bell.

No one could have been happier than I was when I
entered English class first period. I stood by Mrs.
Burr's desk, watching the somber expressions of the
other students who'd entered the room with me. Some
of the poor slobs were still studying, their heads hung
over their textbooks, muttering about gerunds and
noun–verb agreement.

A test paper lay facedown on every desk. After a couple of seconds, while Mrs. Burr ignored me, I decided to take my seat. I waited until the late buzzer sounded. Then, exactly as I'd fantasized, I gathered my books and approached Mrs. Burr's desk. I held out the pink slip. "Guidance wants your signature on this," I told her.

"Really?" She looked at the slip as if it were a dead rabbit. "Well, instead of taking up class time, suppose you come in after school and I'll take care of it then."

"All I need is your signature."

"After school, Huey," she said firmly. "Sit down and take the test."

I glanced at Adam. He raised his eyebrows in mock horror.

I made a silly face at him and went to my desk. Have it your way, Mrs. Burr, I thought. I'll take the test, but I'll talk Miss Cory out of counting it.

Mrs. Burr is famous for her difficult tests, but this was an award winner. Not only did we have to select the proper word or punctuation mark, but to receive full credit for the answer we had to write the reason for our selection. I answered what I could, abandoning my efforts when the passing buzzer sounded.

I spent a lot of time that day fantasizing about my future. I fantasized about winning the Nobel Prize in science, but mostly I restrained myself into daydreaming about having Miss Cory instead of Mrs. Burr for English. I also thought about Megan and Molly and about the expression on Lou's face when I told him that Bass Catcher was at the reservoir again. Remembering that was even better than my fantasy about winning the Nobel Prize.

I asked The Bear to meet Megan at my car after school and explain why I'd be late. Then I stopped by the auditorium to talk to Molly before play practice.

42

When Randall and the other kids in the play appeared, I went on up to Mrs. Burr's room on the second floor.

Mrs. Burr was sitting at her desk correcting papers. As I waited for her to finish grading the one she was working on, I had plenty of time to observe her.

Mrs. Burr really does look like Benjamin Franklin. Her head is roundish, with a high, smooth forehead and a double chin exactly like his. She also happens to have the same hairstyle, rusty-gray hair pulled back in a ribbon at the nape of her neck. She even wears half glasses with wire rims. She put a grade at the top of the test and looked up. "What seems to be the problem, Huey?" she asked.

"No problem," I assured her. "I just need your signature on this." I held out my pink slip.

"Let me see." As she took the paper and scanned it, Mrs. Burr stood, the better to face me. "What is this all about?" she asked.

"Guidance is transferring me to Miss Cory's class."

Mrs. Burr went very still. The she said, "Is there some question as to my teaching ability?"

"No." I shook my head. "Everybody knows you're one of the best teachers at Harrison High."

"Then there must be another reason."

I moved my books from one arm to the other. "My dad was pretty upset over my grade. . . ."

"And whose responsibility was that?"

"It's the tardies and absences," I pointed out. "If you hadn't counted them off my grade, I'd have passed."

Mrs. Burr put the pink slip on her desk while she rummaged through her top drawer. She came up with a dark red booklet, which I recognized as Harrison High's student handbook. She looked at the index, then turned to the information she wanted.

"I am reading from page eight," she said. " 'In order for a student to qualify for a passing grade in any subject, that student must be present and on time for at least sixty percent of the classes involved, regardless of the grade earned for that marking period. Three tardies will equal one absence and any tardiness of over thirty minutes will be considered an absence.' " She paused, then read on. " 'This grading policy is in effect for both excused and unexcused absences, although a teacher may use his/her discretion in the case of excused absences if the student promptly and conscientiously completes the missing assignments.' "

Since I'd get nowhere by arguing with her, I gave Mrs. Burr my best smile and said, "How 'bout giving me a break and signing the slip?"

Mrs. Burr was unaffected by my smile. She dropped the handbook on her desk, crossed her arms, and eyed me sternly over the top of her glasses. "With your ability, you should be a straight-A student," she told me. "The material we covered last grading period was not unusually difficult, but you can't learn if you are not in class."

When I didn't respond, she added, "This is your education we're talking about, Huey. You must learn the tools you'll need for college and your career."

"I'm going to major in microbiology," I pointed out, figuring Mrs. Burr only wanted to make one last pitch for her subject before letting me go. "I don't have to know about gerunds and great literature."

"What about research papers?" Her mouth set in a stubborn line.

"I can learn that from Miss Cory."

"Miss Cory's senior English students write their research papers first semester; my class, second. She and I arranged that system in order to increase the availability of resources to our students."

Small stuff, I told myself. Don't sweat it. "The

44

transfer's already arranged," I said. "I have Miss Panasek's permission and Miss Cory's. All I need is your signature."

"Over my dead body."

I stared at Mrs. Burr, speechless. She'd pulled her chin down toward her shirt collar, making her head resemble that of a turtle about to render himself invincible.

"I mean it, Huey," she said. "I will not give you permission to leave my class. You have an excellent mind and you are going to use it. No tardies, no transfers, and no excuses." Mrs. Burr picked up my precious pink slip. With her eyes fixed on mine, she deliberately shredded it into tiny pieces and dropped the pieces into her wastebasket.

8

The next couple of nights I kept dreaming that Mrs. Burr was chasing me, her arm over her head, hand holding a giant comma like a tomahawk. When she finally caught me one morning at 5:00 a.m., I woke up. I made myself a sandwich and a thermos of hot coffee, then headed for the reservoir. It was a Thursday, but I wanted some space for myself before I faced Mrs. Burr first period.

A blue and white township patrol car was sitting in the parking area. I pulled up beside it, opened my thermos, and sipped coffee. The day promised to be sunny, warmer than normal for late March. A heavy fog was just beginning to lift off the water.

While I was eating my sandwich, there was a tap on my side window. I rolled it down.

"You Lou's S-Team student?" the cop asked. He was young, not a whole lot older than Bear and me. Behind him I could see sunlight breaking through the mist.

"Yes."

"You have the wrong day. This is Thursday."

"I couldn't sleep so I thought I'd check out the birds."

"Then I can leave. Keep an eye out for Benton."

"I thought Lou made him up."

"Benton's real, all right." The cop's grim expression made him look much older. "I ran him off Tuesday."

"What did he do?"

"He was carrying a shotgun. I found a dead heron full of buckshot out here last week. That's a Federal offense."

"Did Benton shoot it?"

"Probably, but I need some kind of proof—a witness, someone to catch him in the act." He straightened, looked out across the water toward the island, then back at me. "My name's Cooper."

"I'm Huey."

When Patrolman Cooper got back into his cruiser and left the parking area, I picked up the binoculars and scanned the water.

Far out, to the left of the island, was a group of ducks, maybe a dozen. They were small and dark, with white cheek patches. I squinted, concentrating on bringing the ducks into clearer focus.

Just when I'd centered in on what looked like a blue beak, the whole group disappeared into a patch of fog. I turned the glasses toward the island.

Bass Catcher stood in shallow water, his head tilted as he stared intently at the water. While I watched, another, smaller heron came in to land near him. Bass Catcher erected his white crest and croaked angrily, then pointed his bill at the sky. He spread his wings, making himself look larger.

At the last moment the other heron swerved and glided across the water toward the parking lot. It fanned its primaries and settled, not twenty yards from my car. The heron was lighter in color than Bass Catcher, almost lavender. It was sleek and slender, reminding me of Megan.

"Little Girl," I said to myself, guessing that the bird was female. If Lou could name a heron, so could I.

As the light grew stronger, more and more herons came to the reservoir. They settled into shallow water and on the banks of the shoreline. Among the last arrivals were two white birds I thought might be albino herons until I noticed their legs were black. I cursed softly; I'd left my bird book at home.

A loud splash diverted my attention from the white birds. Little Girl had caught a fish, small and flat with silver scales. She flipped it over and swallowed it head-first, then paused to eye the Toyota speculatively.

Lou had warned me to stay in the car. "A lot of herons are wary of humans," he'd explained. "They're more likely to accept your car."

I must have been lucky because Little Girl waded several feet closer, then stretched her long neck to peer in my direction. I could see the yellow of her eyes.

She might have come even closer, but at that moment another great blue heron decided to fish in her territory. Little Girl croaked and pointed her bill at the sky, spreading her wings to increase her size. Then, as the invader landed, she hunched over, fixed her eyes steadily on the larger bird, and advanced deliberately through the water toward him.

The other heron croaked too, raising his wings and erecting his crest; but at the last moment his nerve broke. He lifted and flew away, Little Girl close behind.

I was following the chase in the binoculars when I had a horrible feeling I was supposed to be somewhere else. I glanced at the dashboard clock, which hasn't worked in years, then at my wristwatch.

My luck had run out. Not only was I already late,

48

but I could hear the sound of a train whistle in the distance. The whistle meant I'd have to sit while the morning freight train crawled slowly past the road between me and the expressway.

My luck had run out at school too. When I entered Mrs. Burr's room, my test lay facedown on my desk. She fell silent, as did the rest of the class, watching me slide into my seat. My depression deepened when I turned the paper over. I'd scored a big 58.

"Come see me after school this afternoon, Huey," Mrs. Burr told me. "We need to discuss your problem with missing all or part of my class and just what that test grade will mean to you and your future."

9

Figuring my meeting with Mrs. Burr would pretty well ruin the afternoon, I decided to cancel my after-school date with Megan. Like a coward, I asked The Bear to meet her at my car and explain.

"Do you have wheels?" I asked him.

The Bear nodded.

"Could you drive Megan home after you tell her? I promised her a ride."

"Why don't you tell her, Huey? She's starting to call me Bad-News Bear."

"Better you than me." I summoned up a cheerful grin. "I have to meet Molly before I see Mrs. Burr, and I'm running short on time." I looked down the hall toward the auditorium. "She's waiting for me."

As Bear headed for the nearest exit to the parking lot, I wound my way through the mob of students to Molly. She stood near the double doors to the auditorium, her books hugged to her chest, a worried expression in her blue eyes.

"What are you going to do, Huey?" she asked when I came closer.

"Hit the books," I said, acting the noble martyr. "Anything to please Mrs. Burr."

Catching the light note in my voice, Molly said, "This is serious. A lot of colleges rescind their acceptance if an applicant's grades fall."

"You're kidding."

"I'm not. All three places I applied require a final transcript after graduation."

I groaned. "So I'll be spending the rest of my senior year with my head buried in books. It's been nice knowing you."

"This doesn't mean we can't see each other."

"I'll be grounded."

"We'll still be in French together, and we can meet at the library."

"You'd miss the prom to go with a guy who's grounded?"

"You're not just any guy." A smile lifted the corners of Molly's mouth. "Besides, I didn't know we were going together."

"You know you're my best girl," I told her. Then I added, "I'll call you tonight, about seven."

Even the thought of talking with Molly later wasn't enough to raise my spirits as I walked up to the second floor. At the very least, I was due for a lecture on how I was going to shape up or fail senior English.

When I entered the room, Mrs. Burr removed her half glasses, folded them, and placed them on top of a pile of papers she'd been grading. "Pull up a chair, Huey," she said, waving her hand toward an orange plastic chair in the corner by the dictionaries. "Make yourself comfortable while we talk."

After I was seated, she said, "I know you aren't very happy with me right now, but first of all, I'm your teacher rather than your friend. My job is to educate you. If during the process I become your friend, that's fine. If not, at least you'll have learned something. Do you understand?"

"Yes, Mrs. Burr."

"Now." She glanced at her desk, shifted her glasses, and straightened the pile of papers so it was lying parallel to the edge of the desk top. "You missed over forty percent of the questions on the test. That's almost half."

"More than half correct," I said, then closed my eyes tightly. Watch the mouth, I told myself. "I'm sorry," I said when I'd opened my eyes. "I didn't study because I didn't think the test would count in my grade since I was transferring to Miss Cory's class."

"With an F on the first big test, it won't be easy to pull up your average."

She was telling *me* it wouldn't be easy? "Anything you assign me, I'll do," I said. "You won."

"I'd like to think we both won."

Get real, I thought. Out loud I asked, "What will it take?"

"A lot of hard work. You're playing catch-up, Huey. Part of the material covered in the test will be on the final."

"I'll learn it," I told her. "What else do you want?"

"I'm more concerned with what you need, not what I want." Mrs. Burr clasped her hands on top of her desk. "I'm especially interested in your performance on your research paper. To be competent in the sciences, you must be orderly and precise, not only in laboratory work, but also in reports, writing up the details of your research and its results."

Although I didn't answer, Mrs. Burr must have realized from the expression in my eyes that I understood. "This is your last chance to learn to write a research paper before college," she added.

She considered me a long moment. Then she said,

"It would be helpful if I knew why you are late so often for first period."

I could feel blood rising in my cheeks. I looked at my hands.

"I thought you might be into drugs, but according to your records, this is the only class you have a problem with. Are you staying up late nights because of a job? Too much cable television? What's different?"

"I joined the S-Team a couple of months ago," I told her. "I'm helping an old guy in a nursing home, keeping check on some herons for him."

"So?"

"So every Monday, Wednesday, and Friday, I get up at five to drive to Hoover Reservoir. I was late for school once because I fell asleep, and several times I've had to wait for a train at the Conrail crossing. This morning I was so interested in watching the birds, I forgot to check my watch."

"You could bird-watch after school," she pointed out.

I shook my head. "Somebody's been shooting herons early in the morning before there's anyone around. Lou's daughter keeps an eye on them during the weekend, but she drives a school bus during the week. A policeman checks the area Tuesdays and Thursdays. The other days are mine."

"I see." Mrs. Burr leaned back in her chair, studying me. "I think you're going to have to tell your elderly friend to find another person," she told me, "one who's not failing English."

"He already tried. They quit on him."

There was an awkward silence. At the end of it, Mrs. Burr said, "My other section of senior English is seventh period. Could you switch to that class?"

Since both Molly and Randall have English seventh

period, I'd already thought of that. "I can't," I said regretfully. "I have computer science."

"Then you will have to decide which is more important: watching birds or passing English."

Herons had been taking care of themselves for centuries. They'd survive, with or without my help. "Passing English," I said.

Compared with not graduating, great blue herons were definitely small stuff.

10

My predictions to Molly were correct: I was grounded. Both Dad and a yellow deficiency slip were waiting for me Friday after school.

"Don't worry about it," I said, trying to reassure him. "I had a long talk with Mrs. Burr. Everything's all right."

"This is important, Huey." Dad had an expression on his face that said he hadn't realized living with me was going to be so difficult. He also had more gray in his mustache than when he'd moved in the first of the year. "If you fail English, you won't graduate."

"I'll graduate." Despite my words, a shiver ran down my spine and goose bumps rose on my arms.

"I wish I had your confidence." Dad handed the yellow slip to me. "Until I receive a note from your teacher that you have a C average in English, you are grounded. No dates and no other recreational activities."

Luckily, working on my research paper didn't fall under recreational activities. Saturday I picked up The Bear and we headed for the library.

"What if both Molly and Megan show up this afternoon?" he asked.

"No problem," I told him. "Megan's a junior cosmetology student. She doesn't have to write a paper."

"That doesn't mean she can't read."

"She has a baby-sitting job today. She won't be anywhere near the library."

"It *could* happen."

Bear sounded so gloomy that I glanced away from traffic at him. He looked depressed too. His wide shoulders were slumped under his red sweat shirt, and his face was solemn.

"If both girls show up, I can handle it," I told him.

"I just don't want either of them mad at me."

"Why would that happen?"

"Because I knew you were dating both of them and didn't say anything."

"You're my best friend," I pointed out. "Molly and Megan would never expect you to rat on me."

"Then why do I feel guilty?"

"You have an overactive conscience. Relax. Nobody's going to get hurt."

"If they do, I sure hope they don't blame me."

"Besides, I had such a bad week that the law of averages means nothing else can possibly go wrong."

Evidently Bear doesn't believe in the law of averages because he still seemed depressed when I pulled into the library parking lot. On the way to the back entrance, I gave him a reassuring rabbit punch to the shoulder.

"No wonder you're nervous around girls," I said. "You have practically no self-confidence when it comes to relationships with females."

Bear didn't answer. He was busy watching a woman trying to maneuver a stroller out one of the li-

56

brary's double doors and at the same time hang on to a pile of books and a second kid.

"Get a grip on it," I told him. "Be cool like me."

A wheel of the stroller had caught on the edge of the doorway. Bear ambled forward, picked up the stroller, baby and all, and put it down outside the entrance. Then he held the door for the woman and her other child.

It wasn't a woman and the children weren't hers. It was Megan.

"What are you doing here?" I asked.

Megan let go of the older kid's hand to straighten the stack of books she was holding. "I'm allowed," she said. "I'm clean."

"You told me you were baby-sitting all day."

"These aren't the seven dwarfs."

I glanced down at the stroller. The back basket was stuffed with the big, flat picture books little kids like. In front of the picture books, slouched in the stroller's seat, was a baby. Because it was completely enveloped in a pink snowsuit topped by a yellow blanket, all I could see of the baby was round pink cheeks and the yellow pacifier sticking out of its mouth. As I watched, the pacifier wiggled energetically.

The older kid was maybe three or four. It held a book tight against its chest and glared up at me, eyes gleaming with hostility.

"The baby's Shannon"—Megan indicated the pacifier—"and this is Elizabeth."

"Hello, Elizabeth." I gave the hostile one my winning smile.

When she didn't weaken, I added, "My, you're a pretty little girl."

Elizabeth continued to glare. "Is this a stranger?" she demanded of Megan.

"No. He's a friend of mine."

57

"Well, he'd better not touch me."

At that moment the baby spit out the pacifier and began to wail.

Megan put the books she was carrying on the sidewalk in order to pick up the baby. "Pretty Shannon," she whispered into the hood of the snowsuit. "Don't cry." She bounced the bundle of blanket and baby up and down.

The wail decreased in decibels but didn't stop entirely.

Bear picked up the pacifier. "It landed in some dirt," he observed, examining the nipple end.

"Wipe it on your sweat shirt," I told him.

"That won't get rid of germs," said Megan. "Go inside and rinse it in the water fountain."

Bear looked from the pacifier to Megan. I knew exactly what he was thinking because I was thinking the same thing: The Bear, football hero and macho man of Harrison High, strolling into the town library with a yellow pacifier clutched in his hairy hand. I pressed my lips together, trying not to laugh.

The bouncing no longer satisfied the baby. It opened a pink, toothless mouth and screamed.

"Shannon wants her Binkie," said Elizabeth, staring accusingly at The Bear. "Give her back her Binkie."

It was the first time I'd ever seen Bear look completely helpless. He just stood there, uncertain what to do.

"If you're terrified of wrecking your male image," said Megan, "you hold the baby and I'll go rinse off her Binkie."

Bear went to clean the pacifier.

Hoping Molly wasn't watching through a window, I waited with Megan for Bear to return. Meanwhile, the baby screamed at the top of her lungs, and the other kid stared suspiciously at me. I did my best to look harmless.

When Bear reappeared with the Binkie, the sudden silence was like a miracle. The pacifier in the kid's mouth served like a plug in a leaky tire. She stopped crying and the horrible red color in her cheeks faded to pink. She closed her eyes and sucked enthusiastically.

Although I made a quick escape, The Bear didn't. Later I found out he'd walked Megan back to the house where she was baby-sitting. Bear is a lot more tolerant of small children than I am, probably because his oldest sister has three.

Molly was not in the fiction stacks. She wasn't at the card catalog or working on one of the computers either. When I'd given up looking for her and was tracking down resources on cloning for my research paper, I happened on her by accident. She was sitting at a table at the back of the nonfiction stacks, which are located in a mezzanine above the main floor. She was concentrating so intently on taking notes that I watched her for a while without her being aware of me.

What most guys notice first about a girl is her build, her walk, or maybe if she's pretty. What I notice first is hair. That afternoon Molly's hair was like a shaft of sunlight against the dull tan color of the wall. Some of her long curls had fallen forward across one cheek as she bent over her notes. While I watched, she put down her pencil to grasp a lock of hair, twisting and turning it between her fingers as she read.

When I approached her, Molly dropped the curl. "Hi, Huey," she said in a low voice.

Since the only other person in sight was Randall, who was studying at a table at the other end of the stacks, I leaned across the table to drop a quick kiss on Molly's mouth. "I thought you'd gone some-where else," I told her as I sat in the chair across from her. I put the resource books I'd located on the table between us.

"I've been here since noon," she said. "I tracked down books for almost an hour, and the rest of the time I've been taking notes." She rubbed at her neck, then put her arms over the back of her chair and moved to stretch her shoulder muscles.

I made an involuntary sound. Molly couldn't have had more of an effect on me if she'd begun to unbutton her blouse.

"Did you say something?" she asked as she brought her arms forward to rest on the table.

"No, but you shouldn't be allowed to do that in public."

"What?"

"Stretch. If your father knew what I was thinking, he'd press charges."

"You're bad." She smiled at me.

"I try to be." Our knees touched under the table and I thought I'd pass out. When I'd regained self-control, I said, "You want to go for a walk?"

"I thought you were supposed to be studying."

"I did." I indicated the resource books. "Let's get out of here for a while."

"You could take notes from books that can't be checked out of the library."

"I can do that any old time," I told her. "Right now I want to be alone with you."

Molly's knee moved away from mine. "Sometimes I think you just consider me a sex object," she said, "that you don't care one little bit about my personality or my mind."

"That's not true." I was so shocked I spoke at normal volume. When Randall looked up from his work, I lowered my voice again. "You have a terrific personality, Megan. You really do."

"Megan?"

"I meant Molly!" I gulped. "See. You have me so confused I don't even know what I'm saying."

"Who's Megan?"

"The girl Bear's been hanging around with. She met us outside the library. She's baby-sitting a couple of kids. I think Bear's still talking to her."

"Maybe we can double-date with them some night."

"I'm grounded." Thank you, God, I thought. Thank you, Dad and Mrs. Burr.

"I forgot." Molly sighed. Then she said, "I still think you're a lech, Huey."

"Me?" I tried outrage but couldn't quite get it into my voice. Instead, I sounded high and squeaky.

"Maybe an amateur lech, but a lech."

"All men are," I protested. "You don't understand what females do to us."

"And you don't understand what men do to us," countered Molly. A frown began on her forehead, swept into her eyes, and compressed her lips. "I hate it when a guy acts as if I'm nothing but a piece of meat, as if he doesn't care at all about the person who lives inside this body."

I became aware that my mouth was hanging open and closed it. "I'm not like that," I told her. "I just said you have a terrific personality, and I admire your mind too. You're one of the smartest girls in the senior class."

"Nobody ever asked me for a date because of it."

"Well," I said, "you have other . . . ah . . . attributes."

"Yeah."

I couldn't believe what was happening. This was my single opportunity to see Molly during the weekend, and she was acting as if I were some kind of pervert. "You can't tell me that girls aren't interested in sex," I said stiffly.

"I never pretended we weren't."

"Then why—"

"Excuse me." Randall put a hand on my shoulder, tightening his grip until it was almost painful. "Is this a private fight or can anyone get in a few licks?"

"Be my guest," I offered.

"One of the library ladies is headed for the steps to the mezzanine," he told us. "She looks like she's going to kick a couple of loudmouths out in the street."

"They can hear us clear down on the main floor?"

"She isn't coming up here to sell popcorn." Randall gave his easy smile, removed his hand from my shoulder, and went back to his table.

Already I could hear the *clack clack* of heels on the tiled floor at the top of the stairs. I grabbed my books, shifted to the next table, and opened one at a random page, bending over it as if I were reading.

The sound of heels came to an abrupt halt about two feet behind me. There was only the sound of measured breathing: mine, Molly's, and the librarian's. Then, without the slightest hint of anger, the librarian said, "It's a beautiful day. If you two want to have a private conversation, I suggest you go for a walk in the park."

11

Something horrible happened Monday, so horrible it
tied me to Lou and his herons more closely than I'd
ever thought possible. Bad as it was, the whole experience was made worse because of my visit to Lou on
Sunday afternoon.

I tried to tell him about my problems at school, but
Lou refused to listen.

"The next couple of weeks are critical," he told me.
"We're into April. The eggs are hatching." He looked
up at me from under shaggy gray eyebrows. "You'll see
dozens of herons, adults working nonstop to feed their
young."

"I can't watch the herons anymore," I told him.
"I'm always late for my first-period class."

"We're headed into the prime fishing season—for
people too."

"More 'sportsmen' killing herons," I said sarcastically.

"You're outta line, boy!" Lou sat straight up in bed,
the white hair over the top of his head in a wild cow-
lick, reminding me of Bass Catcher with his crest erect.

63

"Fishermen don't kill herons!" His voice was loud and indignant. "*I'm* a *fisherman. Herons* are *fisherbirds!*"

Lou's roommate groaned. He had a clear plastic tube running into one nostril. A similar tube emerged from under his blue blanket to disappear at the foot of his bed.

"Take it easy," I told Lou, afraid he'd have a heart attack.

"Harold Benton is a greedy ignoramus. Harold thinks God gave him ownership of everything."

"What's he look like?"

"Tall and heavy-built, with eyes the size of peas and a brain the size of a beat-up golf ball."

"Peas?" I said. "Golf ball?" Benton shouldn't be difficult to recognize.

"Make it eyes like marbles," said Lou. "Ugliest man I ever saw."

I made acknowledging sounds.

"Tell you what, Huey. You stay on the job two more weeks and you can keep the field glasses."

"I'm not after pay, Lou. You know that."

"At least give me a couple of days to find somebody else."

Ace had wandered into the room, probably attracted by our voices. He walked over to the bed and stuffed his nose into the palm of Lou's hand. Lou patted the dog's head, then fondled his ears while waiting for my reply.

"Get that dog out of here," said Lou's roommate. "I hate dogs."

"Pay no attention," Lou told Ace. "Man's another ignoramus."

"I'll watch the birds until next Sunday," I told Lou. "After that I have to plug in on schoolwork."

As a result of our conversation, I was already feeling guilty when I drove out to the reservoir Monday.

The fact that it was a beautiful, sunny morning didn't help my sour mood. If anything, the crisp, cold air, the birds calmly fishing, and a chickadee scolding in a nearby tree only seemed to point up the ugly resentment and guilt I felt inside.

I located Bass Catcher in his usual territory, then watched Little Girl as she fished the shallow water near my car, working her way past until she was partially obscured by the brush and trees that bordered the far side of the parking area.

There was a lot of duck activity east of the island. As I checked through the binoculars, my bad mood evaporated. Along with a number of mallards, the raft included several hooded mergansers and what might be a wigeon. Beyond them, at the foot of the hill leading to Lou's daughter's house, were three great white egrets. As I watched, first one, then the other two, flew toward me. They veered off at the last moment and headed in the same direction as Little Girl.

She caught another fish, tilted up her head to swallow it, then sipped water. At the sound of the Toyota starting, she looked up to watch me back up and turn. As I left the lot, I checked her in my rear-view mirror. Little Girl was moving farther from the parking lot, behind the trees.

While I slowly eased the Toyota around potholes in the lane, I thought about Little Girl, wondering why she didn't threaten the egrets. Maybe she . . .

KA-BOOM!

The sound ricocheted off leafless trees behind me, so loud and so close it seemed to rock my car.

Little Girl! I rammed the gearshift into reverse and floored the accelerator. The Toyota lurched backward, jolting into and out of potholes, scraping the muffler and brushing against tree branches. It careened into the parking area, almost into the water.

As I jumped from the car, a second shot shattered the silence, followed by an explosion of wings as hundreds of birds took flight. The air itself throbbed and shook with wingbeats and screams of terror. I reached the trees, tripped over a root, righted myself, and ran on. Just ahead was the sound of water splashing and of shrieks more horrible than those of the birds overhead. I burst from the trees and stumbled into the reservoir—knee deep, then waist high in water.

The great white bird screamed and rolled as it tried desperately to rise from the water into the sky. One huge wing clawed at the air; the other was hopelessly submerged beneath the filthy surface. Shreds of feathers pitched and swirled on bloody waves.

The tip of the free wing touched the water, then rose again, stained rust red.

I reached the egret and tried to grab it. It eluded my grasp, slippery with blood, writhing in agony. As I managed to capture it, one pale eye stared at me in horror; the yellow bill fell open.

The bird panted, gasped, and closed its beak. Slowly the light behind the yellow eye went out.

I looked down at the creature in my arms. One delicate black leg hung by a thread of tissue; the foot dangled in the water. The body cavity was torn open, to display black, red, and blue. The beautiful, clean white feathers were broken and torn. All around us pieces of flesh and feathers floated in bloody water.

I hated Harold Benton.

12

A long, hot shower cleaned the traces of blood from my body, but nothing could wash the image of the dying egret from my mind. I paced the floor, going from room to room, staring out windows, until I couldn't deal with thinking about it any longer. I went to school.

Since I'd missed all of first period and part of second, I had to report to the attendance office for an admission slip. Then I went to pre-calc.

Mr. Eldrich was covering new material. Usually I'm interested in math, but that day it took a major effort to act as if I were listening. The sight of the bird twisting in agony kept rising between me and the problems Mr. Eldrich put on the board.

During lunch, Georgette Bayer, a small girl with bouncy brown hair, worked her way through the crowded cafeteria to the table where Bear and I sat.

"Hi," Georgette said when she came within speaking range.

The Bear muttered a hasty "Hi," then devoted himself to reducing his pile of chicken nuggets.

67

"Hello, Georgette." I tried to sound friendly despite the sinking feeling I had inside. Georgette works in the school office sixth period, so I was fairly certain this wasn't a social visit. "What's happening?" I added to make things easier for her.

"This." She handed me a note. "Any answer?"

I scanned the note. Just as I'd suspected, Miss Panasek requested the honor of my presence in her office immediately after dismissal. "Tell her I'll be there," I said gloomily.

"What's wrong?" The Bear asked as soon as we were alone again.

"Miss Panasek wants to see me after school. I was late again this morning."

"Why?"

"You don't want to know." I eyed his chicken nuggets. "At least not during lunch. Do me a favor, Bear?"

"Meet Megan after school and tell her you can't make it."

"Right."

"You know there's a rumor going around about Megan and me?"

"What rumor?"

"That we're . . ."—Bear hesitated—". . . tight."

"Tight?"

"Like going together."

I couldn't help myself; I laughed. "Don't worry," I told him. "I know you aren't."

That was the only laugh I had all day. Every time I remembered my appointment after school, my depression deepened, and not only because of failing English. The bitter fact was that I had failed the egret, too. I'd stupidly assumed that Harold Benton would leave his car in the public parking area and wander along the shoreline blasting away at birds, that he wouldn't even come near the place once he realized someone else had

68

parked there. On top of that, I'd left my post fifteen minutes early, giving him access to the birds with no witnesses.

Miss Panasek's office wasn't as hot as the last time I'd been there, but it wasn't one bit larger. When I'd wedged myself into the chair facing her desk, she left the room for several seconds and returned carrying a straight chair from the outer office. She backed toward the window, the chair between herself and the open door, put it down, and resumed her seat. "Since this problem involves Mrs. Burr, I've invited her to attend our conference," she explained. "If you have any objections . . ."

"No." I was going to have to face Mrs. Burr sometime; meeting her on neutral territory might be easier.

When she appeared, Mrs. Burr looked pretty much as she usually does, except that she'd tucked the tail of her shirt into her skirt. She also was wearing a new layer of bright red lipstick and large gold earrings. They made her look a lot like Benjamin Franklin in drag.

When she was seated, Mrs. Burr opened her grade book to my class. She ran a finger down the list of students, stopping at the fifth name. "Blendenbacher, Huey," she read. "So far this marking period four tardies and three absences, all unexcused."

"Huey?" said Miss Panasek.

"That's right," I admitted.

"Why?"

I didn't answer, only shook my head.

Because three of us were crammed into the tiny space, the room was becoming hot. I was sweating. I tried to look past Miss Panasek to the window, to see outside, but couldn't. I was reminded of a lunar expedition: The three of us were astronauts, floating weightless. I pictured Mrs. Burr's face behind the plastic bubble of a cartoonist's drawing and caught myself before I chuckled.

Miss Panasek was talking about responsibility. One thing for certain, I was a failure at that. The broken leg of the egret, foot dangling in the water, floated into my mind.

"Did you miss first period because you were bird-watching again?" Mrs. Burr asked when Miss Panasek finally shut up.

"I don't want to talk about it." I pressed the heels of my hands into my eyes and swallowed. My throat ached.

"Did something go wrong?"

I kept my hands pressed firmly to my eyes. I was afraid to speak, afraid I'd cry.

There was a long silence, which I used to pull myself together. At the end of it, Miss Panasek suggested that Mrs. Burr leave the two of us alone to discuss my problem.

"I prefer to stay," Mrs. Burr said. "When one of my students is failing, it's my problem too."

What did *she* know about it? The anger that erupted with that thought was so intense it jolted me from my misery. I dropped my hands to give her a sharp look.

"The last time we discussed this," said Mrs. Burr, "you told me you realized English was more important to your future than your project with birds."

"All life is a series of choices, Huey," put in Miss Panasek. "Some choices aren't easy, but they must be made."

Great. Now I had to choose between graduation from high school and my "project with birds." Small stuff. The problem was, the birds weren't small stuff—not to me, not anymore.

When it became clear I wasn't going to answer,

Mrs. Burr said, "I believe I have a partial solution to Huey's problem."

We all know what that is, I thought: Forget "your project."

"I spoke with Mr. Zien, who has Huey for computer science seventh period," Mrs. Burr continued. "Mr. Zien teaches that subject fourth period, when Huey has a study hall. If his computer science can be switched to fourth period and his study hall to first, Huey could take English seventh period."

I blinked.

"Although it won't solve his problem with getting to school on time," Mrs. Burr added, looking at Miss Panasek, "he'll be late for study hall instead of English."

"If you agree, I'll arrange the transfers," Miss Panasek told me.

"*And,*" said Mrs. Burr, looking intently at me, "if you aren't late and don't miss another English class this marking period, I'll ignore your attendance record of the past several weeks."

"You'll do that?" Maybe all wasn't lost. If I did top-level work on my paper and plugged in for the other tests, I could pull out a C. I could graduate after all.

"Only if you are in my room, on time, and present for the entire period every single English class the rest of the nine weeks. *No* excuses."

I raised my right hand as if taking an oath. "I promise," I said, "not to miss any part of any English class for any reason." I meant it too.

13

The first day I had English seventh period, Mrs. Burr was tardy, which never happens, and I mean *never*.

When the late buzzer sounded, the students were in their seats, but the front of the room was empty. At first we were so silent I could hear the sounds of metal contracting in the climate-control system and the rumble of the teacher's voice in the next room. Another couple of seconds passed and Jerrilyn laughed nervously. It was as if we expected Mrs. Burr to crawl out from under her desk and complain because we weren't practicing the parts she'd assigned us for *Macbeth*.

Then the door slowly opened. Randall walked in, his eyes anxiously turned toward Mrs. Burr's desk. When he saw she wasn't there, he let out his breath in a long "Phew," but he still looked very tense.

I wondered why Randall was so stressed out. This was probably the only time he'd ever been late for seventh period, and otherwise he's always been an ideal student.

Then I noticed Randall carried his book and notebook in his left hand. Dangling from his right hand was a very small basket, resembling an Easter basket. I stretched to see what was inside.

The basket was lined with white cotton. In the center of the cotton was nestled a blue egg.

"Man, what's that?" asked Ty Kirksey, a round black kid in the seat next to mine.

Randall peered inside the basket. "An egg," he said.

"I know it's an egg," said Ty. "What are you doing with it?"

Randall shook his head as if to clear it of confusion. "I was on my way here from the cafeteria," he said, "when Mr. Wert grabbed me by the arm and dragged me into his sociology class. He told me this was the day his students were getting married and that there were thirteen girls and twelve boys in his room, so he needed another male."

Ty groaned. Everybody knows about Mr. Wert's sociology class. Every year he performs mock marriages between his students. Then they all play fantasy land about the family unit, figuring out budgets, dividing up household chores, discussing common goals, stuff like that. It's supposed to prepare his students for real life.

"Mr. Wert married me to some white girl I'd never even seen before," Randall told us. "Then he handed me this egg in the basket. He said I have to keep it with me every minute for a week."

"You aren't taking sociology," I pointed out.

"Mr. Wert said that's no problem."

"You should have told him you're too young to get married," said Molly.

"I have Mr. Wert for psychology," Randall explained, "and you know how he is."

We all knew. It isn't that Mr. Wert resents a student who doesn't cooperate; Mr. Wert doesn't believe in resentment. What happens is his feelings are hurt if a student doesn't agree with his plans. Then Mr. Wert becomes depressed. When he's depressed, he gives low grades to everybody; otherwise, he's usually good for an easy A.

Ty leaned back in his seat, as if trying to get as far from the basket as possible. "Do you have to carry that thing over the weekend?" he asked.

"Yeah."

"To the *game?*"

"Mr. Wert said this egg is my child and that a person doesn't get time off from being a parent." Randall raised the basket and peered at the blue egg. "I think it's a boy," he said.

"You could hire an egg sitter," Georgette suggested.

"I could." Randall sounded doubtful. "It's supposed to be a newborn."

"Is it cooked?" I asked, but before Randall could answer, Mrs. Burr entered the room.

If Mrs. Burr noticed Randall was carrying a basket, she didn't mention it. She motioned him to his seat, then waited for the rest of us to become quiet.

"I apologize for being late," she told us. "I was unavoidably detained in the office, not a matter of my choosing."

Seeing guidance wasn't my choosing, I thought. Watching herons wasn't my choice either.

"I know how eager you are to continue with *Macbeth*," she was saying, "but before we do, I have an important issue to discuss."

It was weird, but when Mrs. Burr mentioned *Macbeth*, I realized I was eager to continue work on it. Since I'd read the assignment twice, I was wired.

I was brought back to the present discussion when Mrs. Burr asked, "Could you define *plagiarism* for us, Huey?"

"It's when you copy somebody's words and don't give them credit."

"How is credit given?"

"A footnote or a direct reference in the text." Gotcha, I thought. Won't catch old Huey unprepared, not in English.

"Is that a good working definition of plagiarism, Randall?"

"Yes."

"You don't sound convinced."

Mrs. Burr paused to give Randall time to think. Then she said, "Is it possible to plagiarize an idea? A thought? A theory?" Her eyes cast swiftly around the class. "What about another person's research into the basis for the mutation of plant genes, or the strength of extended family ties in an era of divorce and re-marriage?"

Georgette raised her hand.

If I managed a B on the paper, an A in *Macbeth*, and was in class every single minute seventh period to show my intentions were serious . . .

"Georg—"

"Please excuse the interruption" came over the public address system. "At this time we wish to go over the procedures to follow during a tornado drill."

There was a crackle like paper being shuffled too close to the microphone, then:

"One. All students must leave the classroom in an orderly manner.

"Two. Proceed to the corridor space assigned; face the wall toward the inside of the building, away from windows, doors, and where there might be falling objects.

"Three. Crouch on the floor with your head on your knees and the back of your neck protected by your hands.

"Four. Maintain silence and wait for further instructions."

When the public address system shut off, Mrs. Burr said, "In the case of a tornado drill, line up in single file across the front of the room. We will proceed out the door to the right, to the staircase, following Mr. Greiner's class. We follow them down the stairs to the ground floor, then left along the wall to the corridor outside the doors to the gymnasium." She took a deep breath. "Now, Georgette, what were you going to say?"

Wonk! Wonk! Wonk! Wonk! Wonk! Wonk! Wonk!

I looked at Mrs. Burr. She looked at me. I don't know what went through her brain, but a whole series of pictures flashed in mine. The most vivid was of me as an old man with a long beard and a dunce cap. I was sitting at my desk in Mrs. Burr's room, cobwebs running from my body to the chair. Another image was of me watching the rest of my class dressed in caps and gowns, graduating, and then a vision of myself sitting in a jail cell because I'd plagiarized research without realizing it. The next thing I knew, I was hanging on to my desk top, shouting.

"No!" I shrieked. "I won't go! I'll sue!"

"Huey." Carefully holding his basket a safe distance from me in case I became violent, Randall tugged at my arm. "Come on," he urged. "It's a tornado drill."

I could see Mrs. Burr's lips moving, but I couldn't hear what she was saying. As someone rushed into the room from the hall, I closed my eyes, gripped the desk top more tightly, and screeched, "I'll take it to a higher court!"

"What is the meaning of this?" an unfriendly voice demanded.

I opened one eye cautiously.

Mr. MacWilliams was staring at me from a distance

76

of about two feet. His gray eyes were steely and his jowls quivered with indignation.

My will to resist crumbled. "Sir," I said.

"Get in that line for the drill," he snarled. "At the all-clear signal, you report to me in my office."

"Yes, sir."

It wasn't the way I wanted to meet Molly's father, but then I hadn't planned to meet him at all. I went through the routine of the tornado drill, folded my body into a sweaty ball against the wall in the hall outside the gym, and then reported to the main office.

One of the secretaries behind the counter told me the assistant principal was waiting for me.

Mr. MacWilliams didn't look very welcoming. As he turned his gray glare on me, I felt like curling back into a ball with my hands clasped over my neck to protect it. Instead, I sat in the chair by his desk.

"What's your name, son?" he asked.

I swallowed. "Huey B."

"Huey Bee?" There was a large bloodshot area in his right eye, next to the iris.

"The *B* stands for Blendenbacher. Most of my teachers put a *B* in the grade book because Blendenbacher's too long for the space."

"Are you the Huey who's president of the Key Club and who ran our Grandparents Day program last fall?"

"Yes, sir."

Mr. MacWilliams looked me over carefully. Then he said, "All right, Huey. Suppose you tell me the reason behind the scene over the tornado drill."

"Well . . ."

"Spit it out, son. I don't have all day."

"I've had too many lates to English class, and we were discussing plagiarism, and the tornado alarm interrupted, and we're never going to get back to *Macbeth*." I hesitated, then added, "Sir."

77

"That's it?"

"Yes, sir."

Mr. MacWilliams stared at me—through me—until my hands and armpits started to sweat. At last, when I'd decided we must have been caught in a time warp and were frozen forever, he said, "While I admire your love of learning, I can't help but suspect there is more to the situation."

I rubbed the palms of my hands on my pant legs. "Mrs. Burr and I had a deal," I explained. "If I didn't miss any more of her English classes, she wouldn't count the tardies or absences I already have this marking period. If she includes those in my grade average, I'm going to fail because I already pulled down an F on the first big test."

"I don't understand what this has to do with the tornado drill."

"I promised I wouldn't miss even part of her class for any reason." As I said that, I realized it didn't matter whether Mrs. Burr counted the drill or not. I was doomed. Here I sat in the assistant principal's office while the rest of seventh-period English was learning about plagiarism.

"Tornado drills are the law," Mr. MacWilliams pointed out. "The state has determined the procedure and scheduling of these drills. Every student in every school in our state is legally bound to conform to regulations concerning them."

"Yes, sir."

"Do you understand that the law includes you?"

"Yes, sir." I was beginning to feel like I'd joined the army, but I wanted to be polite.

"Are we going to have any more scenes like the one I witnessed?"

"No, sir."

"You wouldn't want to get a reputation as a troublemaker."

"No, sir." What difference did it make? I thought. What difference did anything make? I wasn't going to pass English this nine-week period, and I wouldn't pass it for the year either.

"Now get out of here before I assign you detention," said Mr. MacWilliams. "Apologize to Mrs. Burr, then report to your eighth-period class."

I obediently stood to make my escape. As I shut his office door behind me, I heard Mr. MacWilliams mutter something. While I wouldn't want to swear to it, what he said sounded like "And stay away from my apple pie."

14

When I left home that evening, most of the sky was still under a cover of clouds, but in the east a full moon was rising. The air smelled moist and sweet, heavy from the spring rain. Life wasn't all bad, I consoled myself. After all, I was meeting Molly at the library. As for my English grade—maybe a miracle would happen.

Randall was the lone male in a group of kids in the hall outside the main lobby of the library. He stood near the coatracks, leaning against the wall, one hand over his head to support himself. His leather bomber jacket was hanging open over a light blue shirt and jeans. There were three girls with him.

Georgette and Teki Thomas were dressed in their cheerleader's uniforms, short, swingy black and red skirts, heavy red sweaters featuring large black letter R's, black sneakers, and red socks. Teki's been Randall's on-and-off girlfriend since our sophomore year. At the present time, I wasn't certain if she was on or off.

The other girl I'd never seen before. She was almost as tall as I am, had beautiful chestnut-colored skin, a short Afro, and the type of build I associate with fashion magazines. She also had huge dark eyes fringed by long lashes.

"Who's your new friend, Randall?" I asked, wondering how he got so lucky and if the dangerous glint I'd caught in Teki's eyes meant trouble.

"Selina Franklin," Randall told me. "Selina, this is Huey B. We go way back."

"Selina's from Boston," said Teki, making Boston sound like the armpit of the universe.

"What happened to your egg?" I asked. Randall wasn't carrying anything except a book, and there was no sign of a basket on the shelves over the coatrack.

"Here." He patted the right pocket of his bomber jacket.

"You have an egg in your pocket?" asked Selina.

Randall nodded.

"Show her," said Georgette.

"Want to see?" asked Randall, clearly enjoying the female attention.

"Sure do," said Selina.

Very slowly, as if he were displaying a precious jewel, Randall removed the egg from his pocket. Cradled in the palm of his hand, it looked very small.

Selina glanced at the egg, then up at Randall from under her long, dark lashes. "I didn't know the Easter bunny was so cute," she said.

Randall grinned happily, but Teki looked ready to detonate.

Selina ran a long, caressing finger over the blue oval, letting her fingertip brush Randall's palm as she drew her hand away.

"Whoo-ee!" Randall executed a series of steps in place. "My baby *loves* that. Do it again."

What happened next could have been an accident, but I doubt it. As Selina's fingers touched Randall's palm, Teki glanced at Georgette, then stepped sideways as if thinking of something to say to her. In the process, Teki bumped Selina hard with one hip.

Selina jerked, her hand striking the egg.

Randall did a quick juggling act, but not quick enough. The egg bounced, rolled, and dropped.

Splat! One second the egg was a solid blue oval. The next it was a mass of broken shell, semisolid egg white, and leaking yellow yolk, surrounded by a circle of feet.

"Oh, no!" said Randall. "And I'd named him Ralphie."

"Ralphie wasn't quite cooked," I observed.

"I knew I shouldn't have taken him from his basket."

"There's egg yolk on my Reeboks," said Georgette.

"Mr. Wert'll kill me," said Randall.

"It's only an egg," I told him. "How mad can he get over an egg?"

"But what will I tell my wife?"

"Wife?" said Selina.

"What a mess." Randall eyed Ralphie's remains.

"It's your kid. You clean it up," said Teki.

That was when I spotted Molly coming in the front doors. I left Randall to his troubles and went to intercept her before she took off her jacket.

"Let's go for a walk," I suggested.

"Now?"

"It's stopped raining," I said, "and I don't want to be stuck inside all evening."

"I have to study."

"Do it tomorrow." My best smile hadn't gotten me much lately, but I tried it on Molly anyway.

"Maybe a short one," she relented.

After stowing our books in my car, we walked down past the post office and the Knights of Columbus, then around the statue of William Henry Harrison, which stands on a terrace in front of city hall. We circled the senior citizens' center and headed back toward the library. We must have walked for an hour, Molly's hand in mine, sometimes with my arm around her.

When we returned to the library parking lot, the moon was hidden by the clouds and big, fluffy flakes of snow had begun to fall. While I unlocked the car to retrieve our books, Molly stood with both hands in her pockets, shivering. I opened the passenger door, reached for the books, then hesitated, looking up at her.

"Let's sit in the car for awhile," I said as if I'd only that minute thought of it.

"I'm cold." Molly shoved her hands deeper into her pockets and stamped her feet.

"It's the wind. You won't be cold inside the car."

Molly tossed her head, her long hair flying away from her face, then took her hands from her pockets and shoved them into her armpits.

"Come on, Molly," I coaxed. "It might be weeks before we're alone together again."

That was all the persuasion it took. Molly didn't object either when I suggested we sit in the backseat where the gearshift wouldn't be between us. She came directly into my arms. Her lips were cold against mine, then soft and warm.

When she slid her head down to my chest, I buried my face in her sweet-smelling hair. I kissed her down across her forehead to her ear. Then I raised her head with my free hand and made a track of kisses down the long column of her throat to nuzzle into the soft hollow where her neck meets her shoulder.

Molly made a faint sound.

There was a bare patch of skin between the waist of Molly's jeans and her sweater. I stroked it, her skin like warm satin beneath my fingers.

83

Suddenly, Molly stiffened, then sat upright. "Who's that?" she said.

I opened my eyes. "Where?"

"There!" She pointed toward the front window on the driver's side of the car.

Since the windows were steamed, all I could make out was the dark silhouette of a head pushed up against the glass. The sight sent a wave of adrenaline coursing through me. I sat up, ready to fight. Then I recognized the shape of the battered old hat my father's been wearing when it's cold and he's not going anywhere important.

"Great," I said. "Terrific."

"Who is it?" Molly asked.

"My father."

"No."

"I guess the party's over." I shoved the back of the front seat forward. "I might as well introduce you."

"I don't want to meet your father like this!"

"I didn't want to meet your father the way I did either." I leaned over Molly to unlatch the passenger door and open it.

Molly and my father were very polite to each other. Dad offered her a ride home, but Molly said her mother had promised to pick her up at nine. She took her books and went inside the library.

"Sitting in the car was my idea," I told Dad as soon as we were alone.

"I don't doubt that for an instant."

"We were only here a couple of minutes."

"I don't doubt that either."

"What are *you* doing here?" I asked, becoming angry.

"We'll discuss that at home."

"You were spying on me!"

"Huey, I am not used to being outside in this

84

weather. I'm middle-aged and getting older by the second. Do us both a favor and come on home where we can discuss this in private."

Driving home, I decided it didn't matter what happened. My life was such a mess that nothing Dad could dream up would make it much worse. I parked beside his car in the garage, took my books, and followed him into the house.

In all the years I'd been spending weekends with Dad, going camping and on our white-water trip, I'd never seen him angry, not at me anyway. I guess that was because both of us were on our best behavior: Dad trying to make me happy, me doing my best to please him. Because of this, I was shocked when he turned on me, his eyes furious, as soon as we'd entered the kitchen.

"I want to know why you were shacked up in the back of your car with some bimbo when you were supposed to be working on your research paper," he said.

"She's not a bimbo," I protested, "and we were not shacked up."

Dad made a disgusted sound.

"It's true!" I told him. "Molly's treasurer of the National Honor Society. She scored a 27 on the ACT."

"And the two of you were studying Shakespeare."

"So I was kissing her! I didn't know that was a capital offense!"

Dad stripped off his coat and threw it on a kitchen chair, then pitched his hat on top of it. He turned in my direction. "Kissing is not what upset me. What upsets me is that you're failing English. In spite of that, you keep playing around instead of settling down to serious work on your paper."

"It doesn't matter what grade I get on that paper," I pointed out. "I could get an A and still fail the nine weeks."

"Why?"

"For one thing, I was late all those times to class, and absent three times. Mrs. Burr said she'd forget that if I promised not to miss any part of English again." I let out a long sigh, only becoming fully aware of the tension in my shoulders as the muscles relaxed. "Then the tornado drill happened, and I had to go see the assistant principal, and—"

"Hold it." Dad put a hand up like a traffic cop. "Are you saying you're failing because of your attendance record?"

"Not entirely." I decided to tell Dad the whole truth. "I didn't learn a lot of the grammar we covered and flunked the first big test."

"Why? You must have a textbook."

"It doesn't cover everything Mrs. Burr teaches, and I'm not exactly gifted in English." I put my books on the table and slumped into a chair.

"Does Bear have this problem?"

"Bear has Miss Cory. Compared with Mrs. Burr, she's easy."

"What about Molly?"

"She's always been a brain in English."

Dad sat down opposite me. He no longer looked angry, only very tried. He rubbed a hand over his face.

"I promised Mrs. Burr I'd never miss even part of class again," I told him, "and then spent practically a whole period at a tornado drill and sitting in the office."

When Dad didn't say anything, I added, "Besides, from now to the end of the year our class won't have English half the time anyway. We'll always be at some dumb assembly."

"Don't exaggerate."

"There are spring sports awards, an assembly for academic achievement, the SADD program on drunken driving before the prom, a movie for our class because we won the exchange-student candy sale, the NHS induction ceremony, and a couple of others."

"I'm amazed you've learned anything at all under those conditions." Dad sounded depressed.

"I just wish I could convince Mrs. Burr I'm serious about bringing up my grade."

Dad frowned. Then he said, "I have an idea."

"I'll try anything," I assured him.

"If you're excused from assemblies, would Mrs. Burr be willing to teach you during those periods?"

"Mrs. Burr would teach *Saturdays* if they let her."

"I'll write one note to the principal, asking for you to be excused from assemblies, and another note to Mrs. Burr, asking her to teach you during those time slots. What do you think?"

Although I wasn't very optimistic, I said, "It might work."

"You'll still be grounded until the grade comes up."

"That's all right," I told him. Dad might not know it, but grounding does have a few advantages.

15

"Congratulations!" said the letter from Ohio Northern. "You have been selected as a member of next semester's freshman class."

"Nice going," Dad told me. "How do you want to celebrate?"

What I really wanted was to call Molly for a date, but I had something to take care of first. "Is it all right if I go out to the reservoir tomorrow after I visit Lou?" I asked.

"Wouldn't you rather take Molly out to dinner and a movie? I'll pay and let you off grounding for the night."

"Some other time." I was determined to solve my dilemma of two girlfriends before it caused trouble between Molly and me. Since there's never a good time to break up with a girl, I decided to get it over with. I called Megan and asked her to go to the nursing home with me and then out to the reservoir.

"Have your chunk of trail bologna?" I asked when I picked her up the next afternoon.

"Ace gets Swiss cheese today."

"Lucky Ace."

Ace wasn't the only one whose luck was riding high. When Megan and I walked into Lou's room, he was alone, sitting in a chair by his bed, reading a magazine.

"Where's your roomie?" Megan asked.

"Went home." Lou grinned. "Now his wife has to put up with the ignoramus." He glanced at me. "How's it going with the herons?"

"All right. Bass Catcher's been showing up every morning."

Lou must have detected some evasion in my voice because he said, "Something bad happen?"

"Benton killed an egret. At least I think it was Benton. By the time I reached the bird, the person who'd shot it was gone."

Lou's lips compressed.

"It was my fault," I admitted. "I figured Benton would park in the public lot, but he must have hidden his car out near the main road and cut through the trees."

"I should have warned you he'd do that."

I'd have felt better if Lou had blamed me. "It won't happen again," I assured him, "not while I'm out there."

Two doors down the hall, in the recreation room, one patient was screaming at another that he'd left the television channel set for the game. "And don't you touch it!" he yelled.

"Fred Frankenthaler," explained Lou. "Fred's not mean, just deaf; and he figures everybody else is deaf too."

Lou must have been right. A woman was protesting in very loud tones that she wanted to watch "Budget Gourmet."

Ace stopped in the doorway of Lou's room, wagging his tail when he saw Megan. After collecting his Swiss

89

cheese, he went on his way in the direction of the recreation room.

At that point Lou's daughter and her children arrived. When an aide stopped by to check on him and
Ace reappeared in the hope of scarfing up more treats,
the room was crowded. Megan and I left for the
reservoir.

There were four other cars in the parking area. A
black man in a green baseball cap was sitting on an
overturned plastic crate at the edge of the water, fishing. Near him, a kid who looked to be in about the fifth
grade was rummaging through a cooler. Beyond the
two of them, her head cocked, staring into the water,
was Little Girl. As Lou'd predicted, fisherman and fish-
erbird showed no hostility toward each other.

"We should have brought a picnic," said Megan.
"We could have invited The Bear to come along and
help eat it."

I didn't answer because I was trying to count herons in the shallow water off the island. Since they kept
moving, it was difficult to keep track of which ones I'd
counted and which I hadn't. Bass Catcher was among
them. He struck the water with a heavy splash and
came up with what looked like a large carp.

Bass Catcher must not like carp. He dropped the
fish, then moved his beak through the water as if to
rinse it.

There were no great egrets mixed in with the other
birds. I wondered if the sight of one of them being shot
had frightened the others away. I scanned the water a
second time but didn't see any large, white birds.

When I lowered the binoculars, Megan was talking
with the kid who'd been rummaging in the cooler. He
was showing her his collection of maggots and night
crawlers. "I have doughballs too," he said. "Catfish like
doughballs."

90

"I should bring Herbie out here," Megan told me. "He'd love this place."

It's amazing how empty a woods seems when there aren't any leaves on the trees. Although most of the trees by the parking lot were only six or seven inches in diameter, they arched thirty to forty feet over Megan and me. Their naked limbs looked black against the blue of the sky.

New leaves were beginning to grow on the bushes that filled the larger open areas of the woods. When we were close to the place where Benton had shot the egret, I got down on my hands and knees and crawled under one. Megan crawled in beside me.

The ground beneath us smelled of wet earth and rotting leaves. It was cold and damp, but a layer of pine needles gave us a dry surface to lie on. "If I can find this spot in the dark, it'd be a good place to ambush Harold Benton," I told Megan.

"You could tie a string from tree to tree and follow it," she said in a quiet voice. "We aren't far from the parking lot."

I rested myself on my elbows and aimed the binoculars toward the patch of water where the egret had died. Not far from the shore was a man in a rowboat. He'd cast a line in the water, but he wasn't watching for bites. He was lying propped up against a seat, his face covered by a straw hat.

A large bee buzzed into the bush, passed close to Megan's nose, and buzzed out again. I watched Megan as she followed the progress of the bee.

I had invited Megan out to the reservoir to tell her that I liked her a lot but that I was going with another girl. Now that we were alone together, breaking up didn't seem so easy. What if she cried? It was such a beautiful day, sunny and warm, not a good day to hurt somebody I cared about.

Megan looked toward me, her face only a few inches from mine, her dark eyes enormous.

I took a deep breath. "I really like you a lot, Megan," I said.

"I like you too."

Her lips were so close to mine. I kissed her.

Megan responded, but after a couple of seconds, she pulled away from me. "Aren't we a little old for making out under bushes?" she said.

I kissed her again.

Megan kissed me back, but when things promised to become more interesting, she broke it off. "Look at that!" she said.

"What?" I mumbled, overcome by a combination of guilt and irritation: guilt because I should have been breaking up with Megan instead of kissing her, irritation because she'd interrupted our kisses. I tried to kiss her again.

"Over there!" Megan tossed her head impatiently. Her hair fanned, tickling my cheek and sending off a cloud of clean scent.

I looked. Then I stared.

Waddling across the open area between us and the water was a very large skunk. The skunk had two white stripes lining the back of its shining black coat. A black and white tail waved proudly over its back like a furry plume.

"That's a really cute skunk," said Megan.

The skunk was cute all right, but I didn't like the way it was approaching. There was a certain determination to the waddle, as if the creature expected to walk right under our bush, maybe even over Megan and me. I remembered that I'd read that skunks don't see very well, that they don't have to since they are protected by the horrible aroma of their spray.

If this skunk did see us, he wasn't worried we might

hurt him. He showed no sign of slowing down as he approached our bush.

"Hey!" I said.

The skunk gave a kind of start, then emitted a squeak much like a mouse.

Megan laughed.

The skunk was not amused. He uttered a louder squeak and stamped his feet. Then he gave a little bounce, the bounce ending with his rear turned toward our bush, his tail high and waving.

I don't remember leaving the bush. I don't think Megan does either. What I do remember is running through the trees until Megan stopped, gasping for air.

She was standing beside a small tree with smooth, gray bark. When our eyes met, she took a final gasp of air and began to giggle. She pointed one finger at me. "Hey!" she said, then grabbed onto the trunk of the tree as she burst into gales of laughter.

The two of us had probably looked ridiculous to the skunk and to any other creature who'd seen us catapult from the bush and run. I threw my arms around Megan and her tree and began to laugh too.

Neither of us could quit. Every time I'd try, I'd have a vision of that indignant skunk, and I'd snicker.

Megan achieved self-control first. "Stop!" she said. Her face was flushed and there were tears running down her cheeks. She gave a little hiccup.

"I'm trying!" I loosened my grip on her and the tree. I couldn't break up with Megan that afternoon. I couldn't bring myself to ruin the laughter.

Besides, Megan is one terrific girl.

16

The next day I was off to the reservoir before dawn. I tucked my car under a tree on the far side of the parking area from the direction I was headed. I crawled out and crossed the lot, looking back over my shoulder before entering the woods.

The morning was cold, with a thick mist that seemed to hover between liquid and ice. I could see my breath steaming through it, but when I looked back, I couldn't see my car at all. Feeling as if I were totally alone in the universe, I walked on in the general direction of the bush I'd chosen.

If the trees had had a full canopy of leaves or the sky had been heavily overcast, I wouldn't have been able to see objects at all. As it was, I made my way to my hiding place partly by sight and partly by touch. I bent down and crawled under the bush.

The motion released a cascade of cold dew, but I was prepared. I'd borrowed an old black raincoat from Dad to wear over my winter jacket. Heavy gloves, boots, and a ski mask helped keep me warm and camouflage my hair and skin. I'd stashed a second pair of jeans in the car in case the ones I wore got muddy.

I waited . . . and waited . . . and waited.

At first I thought about what was going to happen when I caught Harold Benton. Then I thought about Molly and Megan. As time crawled past and cold moisture began to seep through my heavy clothes, I began concentrating on the less pleasant aspects of my present situation.

What if friend skunk decided on a return meeting?

What if Benton thought I was a black bear and shot me instead of a bird?

What if friend skunk brought along his mate for our return meeting?

The ski mask was tickling my neck beneath my coat collar, and I had to blow my nose. It was no easy feat to locate a tissue under all those garments and navigate it to my nose. When I'd finally completed that action and I was busily imagining a brown hermit spider crawling down my left boot to feast on my ankle, I noticed the mist was diffusing. The day was growing light.

Because the spider in my left boot was probably imaginary, I ignored it. I took the caps off the binoculars and aimed at the reservoir.

I could see the edge of the water clearly in the increased light but was unable to locate any birds.

There was a tiny rustling in the wet leaves. Benton?

I realized I was holding my breath and let it out slowly so as not to steam the lenses.

The rustling continued, too minimal to be a man, too large for a mouse. As I watched, a doe emerged from the trees. She picked her way daintily to the edge of the water.

She turned her head and seemed to look directly at me. Her large ears were pricked; her white flag of a tail wagged back and forth, almost like a dog. She gazed back across the water, then slowly moved forward until it lapped around her delicate legs. She lowered her head to drink.

Behind the doe a line of ducks crossed the horizon. I trained the binoculars on them, but they were unidentifiable black silhouettes against orange-colored clouds. When I looked back at the water, the deer was gone.

Herons had begun to come in. They arrived in groups, and they didn't seem interested in defending territories. They immediately began fishing. As soon as they'd caught a number of fish, off they went, leaving room for a new squadron of birds.

Lou had explained this would happen. "As soon as the chicks are hatched," he'd told me, "the adults don't have time to bicker. They'll get there, swallow as many fish as they can, fly back to the nest, and upchuck for the chicks. Then they make another run. They do that from dawn to dark."

Benton didn't appear that day. Fishermen did. Two men accompanied by a springer spaniel glanced at me when I emerged from the woods in my black coat and ski mask. They looked hastily back at their fishing lines, then at each other. The spaniel came to sniff at me and evidently decided anyone with such an interesting scent couldn't possibly be dangerous. It wagged its tail and woofed pleasantly.

When I arrived at school, I went directly to the principal's office with Dad's note and presented it to one of the secretaries.

"Mrs. Hook is in a conference," the secretary told me, "but Mr. MacWilliams should be able to help you."

If Mr. MacWilliams remembered me from our last encounter, he gave no sign of it. He merely read Dad's note and asked, "You want to be excused from all extracurricular activities?"

"Sure," I said recklessly, "if they're during school hours."

"Assemblies? Movies? Pep rallies?"

I nodded. If I wanted, I could attend, but I wouldn't have to. I liked that. It made me feel in control of my life.

"Suit yourself." Mr. MacWilliams initialed the note. "Remember. This does not include fire drills and tornado drills, Mr. B."

On the way to seventh period that afternoon, I showed the note to Randall.

"What's that?" demanded JoJo, grabbing the paper. He read it and said, "Man this is stupid!"

"I like it," I told him.

"Like it?" JoJo called me a very crude name, which Molly, who'd just arrived, pretended not to hear. "You know what will happen? They'll figure if you can miss all this stuff, we can too."

"We won't be that lucky." Randall took the paper from JoJo and gave it back to me.

"We won't be excused from class for *anything*." JoJo glared at Randall, then at me.

"What if we're sick?" Molly asked JoJo. "We can't go to class if we're throwing up."

"They'll make us carry barf bags like on airplanes."

"What happened to Ralphie the second?" I asked Randall. He'd been carrying his basket with a new blue egg during pre-calculus, but now it was missing.

"The project's over. I handed him in to Mr. Wert."

"You don't sound very happy about it," Molly observed.

"My wife noticed Ralphie was a different shade of blue and demanded a divorce."

Hearing the end of Randall's statement as she

97

passed, Georgette told him, "Divorces are nasty. My mother's getting her third."

"The divorce doesn't bother me," said Randall. "I didn't want to marry that girl in the first place."

"So what's wrong?" I asked. Mrs. Burr was standing behind her desk, watching us, but the late buzzer hadn't sounded yet.

"Mr. Wert thinks I'm an unfit parent. He said losing one child and taking home another in the hope my wife wouldn't notice is totally irresponsible."

"He has a point."

"Yeah." Randall didn't look convinced. "Now Mr. Wert's convinced he's a poor teacher," he said, "which makes him depressed . . ."

"Which makes him grade harder," finished Molly.

"All the kids in sociology and psychology are mad at me," said Randall. "Selina's taking psych, and she won't speak to me."

"Hang in there," I was advising when the buzzer went off. I took my note to Mrs. Burr.

Her eyes narrowed suspiciously when she saw the note, but when she'd read it, Mrs. Burr relaxed. "We'll make a scholar of you yet," she told me.

17

On the way to the library that evening, I told The Bear about not having to attend assemblies. "Dad's note gave me a great idea," I said. "I could make a list of all the reasons students are excused from classes and present it to the school board. Maybe they'd get rid of that stupid rule of lowering grades for absences."

"Be sure to put a fractured skull on your list" was Bear's only comment.

"Who has a fractured skull?"

"You will when Molly and Megan find out you're going with both of them."

"No problem," I assured him. "If Molly and Megan haven't found out by now, they aren't going to."

Bear muttered, "Wanna bet?"

"Girls will do practically anything to avoid a confrontation," I explained as we entered the building. I waited while he drank from the water fountain, then continued talking as we passed the entrance to the children's room and the main desk. "Girls hate a big scene with yelling and hurt feelings. Even if Molly or Megan does find out, the most she'll do is cry a little."

We rounded the card catalog.

"Th—" I ducked behind the card catalog.

Bear kept walking.

"Bear," I said in a loud whisper.

"Hunh?" Bear stopped in his tracks, looking around as if I'd vanished into thin air.

"Over here."

Bear returned to the card catalog, standing close enough to talk to me, but where he could see the tables near the magazine section.

"Molly and Megan are here!" I said. "They're sitting at the same table!"

"Where?"

"Near the magazines!"

"Oh, yeah," said Bear when he spotted them. "You just told me girls will do anything to avoid a confrontation, so what's to worry about?"

"I said *practically* anything." I was tempted to peek from behind the card catalog but thought better of it. "What are they doing?" I asked.

"They're waving at me." Bear got a big, sloppy smile on his face as he raised the hand that wasn't wrapped around his books to wave back. "Which one of them are you going to dump, Huey?"

"I'm not going to *dump* anyone," I said. "What are they doing now?"

"Molly's taking notes. Megan's watching me." The Bear was peering around the edge of the card catalog at me. "You haven't seen much of Megan lately. She'll probably recover fast if you break up with her."

"Are you kidding? Megan is crazy for me."

"Then that leaves Molly."

"No." I stared at a card catalog drawer, a bare two inches from my face. The label on the drawer was NE–NO. "Listen, Bear," I said. "You go distract Megan. Lure her away from the table."

100

"How?"

"Tell her someone big is in the parking lot."

"Like the Refrigerator?"

"No! Not a football player. Somebody she'd like, maybe Michael Jackson or Tom Cruise. While the two of you go look for him, I'll get Molly away from the table."

As Bear turned to walk away, I said, "Wait!"

He turned back.

"Make it believable, a person who might actually be in town."

"Who?"

"Think of somebody."

I gave The Bear five seconds, then sneaked from behind the card catalog to the safety of the wall below the stairs to the mezzanine. I circled behind the staircase, passed the science fiction and romance books, and went down the line of stacks that hold regular fiction. At the COS–DEL stack I headed toward the magazine section, stopping when I located a convenient space between books to watch Bear and the girls.

"How long have you been talking to card catalogs?" Megan asked him.

"A couple of weeks," said The Bear. "Do you want to come out to the parking lot for a minute?"

Megan cocked her head as she looked up at him, her shiny brown hair brushing one shoulder as she moved. "I don't think so," she said. "I'm studying."

"E.T.'s out there."

Molly laughed, but Megan only stared at Bear, one dark eyebrow drawn up into a question.

"Er, I meant the mayor," said Bear.

"Why would I want to see the mayor?"

"The Cookie Monster?"

"What's with you, Bear?"

"I'm trying to lure you away from the table so we

can have a private conversation, but I don't know how to do it."

"That's for sure."

I should have known better than to send Bear. Instead, I should have asked the lady at the desk to page Megan. I was about to sneak back to the main desk when Megan shoved back her chair and stood. "This had better be good," she said.

I gave them a chance to get out of sight, then strolled casually up to the table.

"Hi," said Molly as she looked up from her work. "I was beginning to think you'd gotten lost."

"I'm here now." I gave her what I hoped was a charming smile and added, "Let's go somewhere else, Molly. I have something private to tell you, something important."

"I'm three assignments behind in French," Molly protested. "If I don't hand them in tomorrow, Mrs. Bartolli won't give me credit for them."

"It'll only take a minute. We don't have to leave the library."

"So tell me here."

I was beginning to sweat. Since I had my back to the direction that Bear and Megan had gone, they could be headed back our way and I wouldn't see them. "Come on up to the nonfiction stacks," I said.

"Why?"

"Because I asked you to."

Molly sighed heavily, but she stood.

Not daring to glance toward the main desk, I hurried to the stairs and up them. I didn't relax until Molly and I were safely located in the section on travel books. Then I leaned against the partition between shelves and let the tension drain out of me.

"What did you want to tell me?" Molly must have been serious about working on her French. She held her textbook open against the front of her blue sweater, as if it were a magic shield between us. She also carried the yellow pencil she'd been writing with.

"Mrs. Burr will have no regrets that she gave me the part of Banquo in *Macbeth*," I told her. "I've practically memorized his lines."

"Is that all?"

"Of course not. I wouldn't bring you all the way up here just to tell you that," I said, thinking rapidly as I moved away from the partition, closer to Molly. "I'm starting a campaign to change school policy."

"How?"

"I'm making a list of all the reasons the school excuses students from class. When I'm done, a group of kids can present the list to the school board, so they'll realize lowering grades for absences is totally unfair."

When Molly made no comment, I added, "This is big, Molly, really big."

"You think so?"

I leaned closer. "A lot of things could change because of me and my list. The school system will have to do away with most of the stupid assemblies we go to."

"Like the one featuring scenes from the school play."

"Not something important like that."

"You're going to get tornado drills eliminated," she said sarcastically.

Molly had missed my point. Deciding she'd understand if she was involved in my efforts, I asked, "Will you help me?"

"No."

"We can . . . No?"

"Aren't you forgetting something, Huey?"

"What?"

"My father's assistant principal at Harrison High.

How will it look if I'm part of a demonstration against school regulations?"

"It isn't a demonstration. You wouldn't have to carry a sign."

"You might not like him," Molly said, her blue eyes icy, "but my father happens to be a very nice man."

"I like him," I said. "I think he's terrific."

"It's really hard being assistant principal. None of the kids understands how tough his job is."

"I admire your father," I told her. "Honest." This was not working out the way I thought it would. I decided to reason with her. "Everyone would benefit from my plan," I said. "You, me, the other students, the teachers and administration too. Your dad probably hates the way students are always being pulled out of classes."

"He says if he were in charge, things would be different," Molly conceded.

"See? Find out if your father agrees with me. If he doesn't, I won't expect you to help me. I only told you what was happening because I'm not the type of person who'd do anything behind your back."

"I know you aren't." Molly's voice softened. "I'm sorry I snapped at you. Between play practice, my research paper, and trying to keep up in my other subjects, I'm really stressed out."

"That's all right." Molly was so pretty, and we were alone. I leaned over—

And became aware of a pair of large, dark eyes, filled with fury, staring at Molly and me through a gap in the travel books on the next shelf.

As I straightened, Megan charged around the end of the stacks. "Exactly what do you think you're doing, Huey Blendenbacher?" she demanded. Her normally pale complexion was flushed angry red. Her eyes flashed fire. Behind her, The Bear lifted his hands in apology.

"I was . . ."

"What's going on here?" Molly looked from Megan to me.

"Nothing," I said.

"It just so happens that *your* boyfriend is *my* boyfriend too," said Megan.

I made a small protesting sound.

Megan glared at me. "You did tell me I was your best girl, didn't you, Huey?"

"But that's what he told me," said Molly, "that I was his best girl."

Megan stopped glaring at me to look at Molly. She ran her eyes over Molly's lush shape, then said, "He told me I have a perfect figure."

"He told me hugging a skinny girl is like hugging a bundle of bones," Molly retaliated.

I groaned. In another two seconds the girls would be exchanging blows instead of words, rolling around on the floor, scratching and biting, fighting over me.

Molly had moved closer to Megan as she spoke, her fingers tightening around her pencil. I put a hand on her arm, afraid she might use the pencil as a weapon.

Molly wheeled. "Don't you dare touch me!" she said.

I jerked my hand away as if it had been burned.

"I hate you, you rotten scumbag," said Megan.

At that point I became aware of someone standing behind me. "I'm afraid I must ask you people to be quiet," came another female voice from the vicinity of my left ear. "The library is not the place to discuss personal problems."

Since I didn't want to see the expression on the librarian's face, I didn't turn around. I didn't want to see Molly's or Megan's expression either. I closed my eyes

105

tightly until I heard them move away together, talking about me. When I ventured to open my eyes again, I was alone except for The Bear.

"At least you didn't end up with a fractured skull," he told me by way of comfort.

When I didn't answer, Bear gave me a friendly slap on the back. "Cheer up, Huey," he said. "This way you don't have to decide which girl to dump. They both dumped you."

18

When one male is mad at another, quite often he tries to do the offender immediate physical damage. Or he might wait until later, say after a game. Then the two of them fight it out, leaving each other covered with lumps and bruises but relieved that the difference is resolved.

If there are serious problems between them, males sometimes make a series of forays against each other. One might round up a group of his friends, lie in wait for the enemy, and attack. They'll beat the victim to a bloody pulp. I think that's why women seem to suspect that deep inside practically all men are barbarians, that we cause the wars, most of the crime, and every other thing that goes wrong in the universe.

Personally, I believe men are straightforward and honest in dealing with their differences. If some guy's looking at me with murder in his eyes, and I ask, "What did I do?" he'll say, "Tried to steal my girl friend." Then he'll pop me a good one. If he's a lot bigger than I am, he might not have to pop me; he'll just glare like an angry gorilla until I get the message. Either way, the whole matter's settled in a couple of minutes.

Women prefer to draw the pain out over a period of time. This can last so long their victim can't remember what he did wrong, or maybe he never knew in the first place. He's only aware that this female is looking at him with sad, accusing eyes. Not only that, a lot of other girls are looking at him the same way, whispering when they see him in the halls, talking behind his back, agreeing that he's exactly what they suspected all along—a coarse, unfeeling barbarian.

I'd bet anything the first guerrilla fighter was a woman. I'd also bet she never had to lay a finger on her enemy. From past experience I realized the next several weeks were going to be pure misery.

I figured Megan wouldn't be much of a problem since I hardly ever run into her at school. Besides, Megan seemed to take a guy's approach to expressing her opinions. Since she'd called me a rotten scumbag, she probably didn't think about me at all anymore.

Molly was a different matter. In addition to being in Mrs. Burr's class together, we have French the same period every day. With Molly sitting three rows ahead of me, it was very difficult to concentrate on French. I stared at the back of her head and tried to think of ways to let her know I was sorry. I'd promise myself I'd apologize at the end of class, but I didn't. Whenever Molly's eyes met mine, hers contained a cold, disinterested expression that made the words die in my throat.

To make matters worse, Molly and Megan had the same lunch period. I know because Randall is in there with them. The Wednesday after the big blowup, he stopped at my desk on the way into pre-calc. "You have trouble," he said.

"Tell me about it." I meant to be sarcastic, but evidently Randall didn't notice.

"Guess who's getting real close."

At first I thought Randall meant himself and Selina, but there was no way their relationship would hurt me. "Who?" I asked.

"Molly and Megan. I saw them together in the cafeteria yesterday."

"At the same table?"

"Side by side, like sisters. They were acting like it was a party."

"Thanks for the warning."

"Any time."

That was bad news. With my usual optimism, I'd hoped that after a couple of rocky weeks Molly would forgive me. I'd make it up to her by taking her to the prom, then out to dinner afterward at an expensive restaurant. If Molly and Megan were close friends, my chances of dating Molly again were practically nonexistent.

At least I didn't have lunch the same period as the girls, didn't have to see them talking and laughing at me. I'd never have to deal with the two together face-to-face. That's what I told myself, anyway.

As a matter of fact, I was telling myself that later the same day, on the way to the public telephone in the main lobby. We had a substitute in physics, a man who knew less than I did about the subject. He'd given the class a study hall and made no objection when I asked for a pass to go use the phone.

That morning at the reservoir I'd run into Patrolman Cooper, who'd located the heronry where Bass Catcher had a nest with three chicks. "They all look fat and healthy," he'd told me.

Since I'd finished my homework, I decided to call Lou with the news and also to tell him I'd increased my heron runs from three a week to five. Most mornings I woke up automatically by four-thirty and was usually out at the reservoir under my bush by five. No way was Benton going to slaughter any more birds, not while I was guarding them.

Thinking of herons and wondering if the young ones would fish at the reservoir when they'd fledged, I crossed the intersection of halls at the offices. I was headed for the phone when I happened to glance in the direction I was walking.

Not ten yards away, coming directly toward me, were Molly and Megan.

I pushed open the nearest door and ducked inside. The disaster of running into the girls loomed so large in my mind that it took me almost ten seconds to figure out where I'd taken refuge.

Of course, I'd realized right away I was in a lavatory. The tan, tiled walls and the smell told me that. From the small entryway, my eyes roved over a row of sinks, a long steel shelf above them, and across the bank of mirrors over the shelf. On top of the center mirror was written in red lipstick: JASON SCOTT IS GNARLY. My eyes flickered on and came back.

Lipstick! I was in the *girls'* lavatory!

I'd reached the door, my hand flat on it to push, when I realized this maneuver would bring me face-to-face with Megan and Molly. As I hesitated, a nearby toilet flushed.

Sweat popped out on my forehead. Then I figured the sound was too far away. It had to have come from the boys' lavatory next door. I listened intently. I couldn't hear any noise coming from within the girls' room, nor could I hear footsteps approaching outside.

Give them ten seconds, I told myself, and began to count under my breath. "One-and, two-and . . ."

At "seven-and," a low giggle came from the other side of the door. Another giggle, more highly pitched and louder, joined it. The giggles were followed by a whispered conversation. The door to the girls' lavatory swung slowly inward.

For one wild second I considered taking refuge in a toilet cubicle. Then I wheeled to face the tile wall, leaning my forehead against it. Behind me, two people entered the lavatory. The door closed.

"Why, who is this in the girls' lavatory?" said a high, bright voice, belonging to Molly.

"It must be a new girl in school," said Megan. "What's wrong, honey? Don't you know your way around?"

"My, is she ever tall!" said Molly. "What's the weather like up there?"

For one awful second I thought I'd burst into tears. Then I felt a terrible heat, as if all the blood in the top half of my body had rushed to my face. I pushed past the girls and ran out the door, directly into a person passing in the hall.

"Hold it, son." A hand held me upright. It also prevented me from escaping.

"It's Huey B," said Miss Panasek.

"Coming out of the girls' lavatory," Mr. MacWilliams added. "What were you doing in there, Huey?"

"Nothing, sir."

"You had to be doing something," Miss Panasek pointed out.

At that moment I hated women, all women, with the barest exception of my mother. "Making a mistake," I said in a choked voice.

Miss Panasek lifted her eyebrows. Mr. MacWilliams let go of my arm to run a hand over his short hair. "You'd better have some explanation," he said.

"I was trying to get away from a couple of girls."

"By hiding in the girls' lavatory?"

"Yes, sir."

"Would you like to come to my office and discuss it?" said Miss Panasek.

Except for running into Molly and Megan again, the last thing I wanted to do was go to Miss Panasek's office and discuss it. Besides, by that time my throat had closed so tightly I could hardly speak. I opened my mouth as I tried to think of a polite way to refuse.

"Never mind," Mr. MacWilliams told Miss Panasek. "I'll take care of this."

"But I'm his counselor."

"I will handle it." Putting a hand on my shoulder, Mr. MacWilliams propelled me down the hall, away from the guidance office, toward administration. When we arrived at the entrance to his office, he gave me a swift pat on my shoulder and dropped his hand.

"Go on back to class, son," he said. "It's safer there."

19

When Mr. Eldrich made arrangements for me to be excused from first-period study hall in order to monitor wildlife at the reservoir, I threw away the list I'd been making for the school board. The dawn patrol was so important to me I'd be stupid to risk it in a protest over absences.

At times I wondered if there was something wrong with me. I was a senior in high school, a normal male with normal drives, and the biggest pleasure in my life was crawling under a bush, in the dark, by myself, at an hour when most kids my age were still asleep—if they'd gotten home from the party yet.

When I asked my dad if he thought I was weird, he said, "No. I think you're one of the lucky people."

"How?"

"You know what your interests are, what you want to do with your life. Most people don't find that out until they're adults." He paused, then added, "A lot of us go through life in jobs that don't really matter. We're only putting in time for money."

"I think selling insurance is important," I told him.

Dad gave a snort, then smiled. "Thanks," he said. "I guess in a way it is." Then he added, "I'd like to tell you something else."

"What?"

"I'm glad your mother married that yuppie and moved to Chicago. She gave me a chance to get to know my son."

I'm glad Dad feels that way, especially since I can't help noticing his hair is a lot grayer now than it was when he moved in with me in January.

Early morning became my thinking time. While I waited for day to dawn, for the deer or a skunk or the herons to appear, I'd lie under my bush and mull over how ironic it was that Molly and Megan had become friends and how The Bear had signed for a full scholarship to play football at Michigan but didn't get a swollen head over it. I'd wonder what my college classes would be like, and I decided to specialize in either environmental studies or ornithology instead of microbiology. One early morning I even realized why Mrs. Burr is so passionate over *Macbeth* and fusses over grammar and punctuation. For Mrs. Burr, a comma is like a microbe, and a play like *Macbeth* must resemble a perfectly balanced ecosystem.

A few minutes after I came to that conclusion, I met Harold Benton. My mind had turned from Mrs. Burr to Molly. On the way out of class the day before, she'd brushed my arm. She glanced at me, blushed, and quickly looked away.

I'd wanted to tell Molly how terrific she'd been reading Lady Macbeth's part and to apologize for going out on her. Most of all, I wanted to ask Molly to give me another chance, but the words stuck in my throat. I kept remembering the scorn in her eyes in the library stacks and the way she and Megan had teased me when I ducked into the girls' lavatory.

Although I was engrossed in my girl troubles, the part of my brain that registers sound picked up a stirring in the leaves. Expecting a deer to emerge into the clearing by the water, I retrieved the binoculars and propped myself on my elbows.

"*Quack, quack, quack*" came from the water. "*Quack, quack.*"

Mallards, I figured, but since I'd spotted a pair of wigeon earlier in the week, I zeroed in on the creature making the sound.

It was a mallard, all right, a female in the company of a male, another female, and two great blue herons. Although they were only a few feet apart, the herons were ignoring the mallards. They stood with their heads cocked, staring into the water.

I was attempting to determine if the heron on the right was Little Girl when more rustling in the leaves reminded me of the doe. I swung the binoculars to the left, expecting to focus in on a tan coat, delicate legs, and ears pricked for signs of danger.

I focused on a tan coat, but it was flat instead of soft and furry. I lowered the binoculars to look over them.

Harold Benton was built blocky and he was big, not just tall like me, but heavy too. Because his back was toward me, I couldn't see his face. His hat was pulled down over his hair, so I couldn't see that either. He was wearing dark pants and a hunting jacket, but the jacket didn't have a license pinned on the back.

I wasn't even certain the man was Benton. I hesitated, undecided if I should draw attention to myself. I would feel like a fool if I crawled out from under my bush to challenge an innocent man.

I didn't see the double-barreled shotgun until Benton raised it to his shoulder.

Once when I was a little kid, I'd touched a strand of electric fence. The surge that shot through my body at the sight of the gun had the same effect. I dropped the binoculars and burst from the bush—too late.

An explosion seemed to detonate inside my head. Then I was across the clearing. I threw myself at the gun.

I grabbed the barrel, sending the second charge into the air past my head. There was a blast of heat in my hands, then the smell of scorched hair. I felt a terrible pain in my left ear.

I wrenched the gun from Benton.

The birds must have panicked, screaming and splashing as they took flight, but I was unaware of them. I faced off with Benton, raised the shotgun, and swung it like a club toward his head.

At the last moment I realized what I was doing. I swerved, spun, and threw the gun as far as I could into the reservoir.

Something heavy struck me square in the center of my back, knocking me facedown into the reservoir. Benton straddled me, his legs locked around my waist, his hands scrabbling at my head. He grabbed my hair and forced my head underwater.

I twisted violently, pulled my legs under me, got purchase on the slippery bottom, and pushed upward.

When my head broke the surface, I grabbed air, but I was shoved under again. I groped in the water, caught hold of a foot, and pulled. Benton's shoe came off in my hand.

After that, everything began to run together in a blur. Behind my eyelids, I saw black, then brilliant red. My fight with Benton blended into a struggle against the water and against my own body's impulse to breathe water into my lungs. I was barely conscious when I sensed a terrible weight being lifted from me.

Then I was being dragged from the water by the

back of my coat and dumped on the ground. I retched, pulled air into my lungs, and retched again.

"You all right, Huey?" demanded Patrolman Cooper.

"Yeah." My ear hurt; my whole head ached. I was shivering uncontrollably. I opened my eyes to look at the water. The surface was flat, with no sign of blood or feathers. I felt great.

"I paid five hundred dollars for that gun!" yelled Benton.

"You won't be needing it," Cooper told him. "You know how lucky you are?"

"Lucky?" Benton's mouth fell open. He looked ridiculous: soaking wet, his hat missing, and his hair plastered to his head. One shoe was gone; the other was a ball of mud. Like Lou said, his eyes were small and mean, but he still looked dangerous.

"If I hadn't heard the shots, you'd be facing murder charges," Cooper told him.

After that, Benton was silent. He didn't even protest when Cooper put handcuffs on him and loaded him into the back of the cruiser.

His prisoner stowed, the patrolman came over to where I was standing near my car. "Are you sure you're able to drive?" he asked.

"I'm all right."

"Promise you'll stop at the emergency room."

When I didn't answer, he added, "It's important, not only for your benefit. The court will need the hospital record of your condition when Benton goes up before a judge."

"I'll go to the emergency room," I told him, "and I won't go home to clean myself up first."

"Good," said Cooper. "Good job, Huey."

On the way to the emergency room I drove past Middlebury Manor. I turned in a driveway and went back. I parked the Toyota and went into the nursing home.

Lou wasn't in his room. The nurse behind the main desk on his hall looked a little startled by my appearance, but when I asked for Lou, she directed me to the recreation room. She did follow me down the hall, I guess to make certain I didn't give him a heart attack.

The television was tuned to a game show, but no one was watching it. Four men were playing cards at a table in one corner of the room. At another table several women were making what appeared to be doll clothes. There were two people in wheelchairs, one asleep, the other reading a book.

Lou was sitting near a window, holding a newspaper and talking to a woman on a nearby couch. He broke off as I approached. "You met Harold Benton," he said.

"Right."

Lou grinned. "From the way you look," he said, "and from the expression on your face, I take it Benton was not pleased to make your acquaintance."

"Right again." I smiled. "The herons didn't lose a feather," I told him, "and Harold Benton is sitting in the county jail."

20

Since I didn't want to run into Molly or Megan at the Youth Center, the first Saturday night I wasn't grounded I arranged to meet The Bear at Fast Lanes. He strolled into the bowling alley shortly after nine, threw his athletic jacket on the seat of the chair next to mine, and collapsed on the chair opposite me. It creaked and swayed under the sudden weight, but held.

"I stopped at the Youth Center," said Bear. "The band didn't show, so Mike Howard's pretending he's a DJ." The Bear made a face, as if he were going to puke.

"Were Molly and Megan there?"

Bear ignored my question. "I still think we should have gone to a movie," he told me. "This is the last night for *Gangrene*."

"Face it, Bear. Going to a movie with you is not like going with a girl."

"It's cheaper," he pointed out.

"So's bowling."

"Especially when all the lanes are taken."

"There's only one other group ahead of us."

"Then I'd better rent shoes and a ball," said Bear. "You want anything from the snack bar?"

I shook my head, watching the bowlers. A girl in lane eleven reminded me of Molly, but this girl was wearing her long blonde hair in a pigtail. She was built like Molly and about the same height.

When Bear returned to our table, he put the bowling ball and shoes on top of his jacket, then left again, headed for the snack bar.

"Bring me a vanilla shake," I called after him, changing my mind.

Fast Lanes is the biggest bowling alley in our town and the newest. In addition to having twenty-six lanes and computerized scoring, it has a room called The Lounge, which is an area of tables and chairs separated from the lanes by a long, low wall. The table I'd claimed for The Bear and me was behind lanes fourteen and fifteen.

An elementary school kid was bowling in lane fourteen with an old lady. The kid, who reminded me of Megan's brother, would walk to the foul line, bend his knees, and throw the bowling ball. The ball would land with a thud and wobble to the closest gutter. This didn't bother the kid. After every toss, he'd make a fist and wave it over his head like he was a national hero.

When Bear returned with my vanilla shake, I pulled a couple of bills from my pocket and threw them on the table. He made change, sliding a quarter and some pennies toward me, then settled into devouring a pile of French fries.

"What is it you like most about girls?" he asked when he'd reduced the pile to half its original size.

"They're pretty." I watched the old lady with the kid pick up her ball, balance it in front of her, then move briskly toward the foul line. The man in the next lane carefully wiped his hands with a towel before his turn. Both of them scored strikes.

"What else?" asked Bear.

"They smell good."

"I don't?"

I glanced at him. He was wearing his BE MORE LIKE BEAR sweat shirt and was busily stuffing the last of the French fires into his mouth.

"They have better manners than guys," I said.

Bear grunted.

"What I really like about girls," I added, "is that girls like to hear about me. Guys only want to talk about themselves."

Bear grunted again. Then he said, "Megan dyed her hair."

"She did?" I thought of Megan's beautiful dark hair. "Why'd she do that?"

Bear shrugged his massive shoulders. "She didn't dye all of it," he said, "just part."

"Where'd you see her?"

"Around." Bear looked at his watch, then toward the front entrance to Fast Lanes.

"We don't have much longer to wait," I told him. "The group before us got a lane while you were buying food, and the old lady with the kid can't hang on all night."

"When are you going to make up with Molly?" he asked.

"Maybe never," I said. "We'll be going away to college soon anyway."

"Like in four or five months."

"Do you mind not talking about this?" I asked. "We're supposed to be having fun."

"I want you to be happy," he told me. "Why don't you apologize?"

"I tried, but the words got stuck in my throat."

121

"Send her roses," suggested Bear. "My dad does that after he and my mom have a fight."

What a switch—The Bear giving *me* advice about girls. He wiped grease from his fingers onto a paper napkin, glancing toward the entrance again as he did so. When a relieved expression crossed his face, I turned in my chair to see what caused it.

Megan and Molly stood on the mat inside the double doors. As I watched, Megan brushed her shoes on the mat. Molly took off her red jacket.

"You set me up!" I said to Bear.

"You have to make up sometime. A man can get in trouble hiding in girls' lavatories."

"What'll I do?" I asked as the girls came toward us. "What'll I say?"

"You're next," interrupted a middle-aged man. "You want the lane?" He jerked his thumb toward lane twenty.

"Go ahead," Bear told him.

"You should have warned me," I muttered as the girls closed in on us.

"Relax," he said.

"Mind if we sit down?" asked Megan. Since she'd begun clearing shoes, bowling ball, and Bear's coat off a chair, there wasn't much point to her asking.

"Hello," said Molly.

I mumbled, "Hi," then glanced at Megan. She'd dyed the bottom two inches of her hair orange, cut straight bangs across her forehead, and dyed the bottom fringe of them orange too. The result looked a lot like kitchen curtains.

"Want to go to the snack bar?" she asked Bear as she draped his coat over the wall between us and the lanes.

"I already ate a double order of French fries and a candy bar."

"Bear . . ."

"Oh, yeah," said Bear. "That's right. Sure."

I was alone with Molly, as alone as we could be at Fast Lanes on a Saturday night. Summoning courage, I looked directly at her.

She was watching me.

"I apologize for seeing Megan behind your back," I told her. "The first couple dates, I figured it didn't matter. By the time we were going together, I didn't want to hurt either of you."

"So you hurt both of us."

"I'm sorry."

"I'm sorry too," said Molly. "Megan and I shouldn't have teased you."

"I deserved it." The muscles in my arms and legs loosened. I wiped the palms of my hands on my jeans. As Molly smiled, I remembered how soft and warm her lips were on mine. "I really meant it when I said you're my best girl," I told her.

"What about Megan?"

"She's okay as a friend," I said cautiously. "She's pretty pushy at times."

"I like her," said Molly. "Megan's assertive, but there's nothing mean about her."

Since I wasn't comfortable discussing Megan with Molly, I changed the subject. "Will you go to the prom with me?" I asked.

"Aren't you grounded?"

"Not anymore."

"I'd love to go to the prom with you," said Molly.

That was when Megan and The Bear returned. The Bear was carrying a bowling ball and shoes. Megan balanced three soft drinks. "I didn't know your size," she told Molly, "so we couldn't rent shoes and a ball for you." As she leaned over to place the soft drinks on

123

our table, Megan's two-toned hair swept across her cheeks.

"Can you bowl?" I asked Molly.

"Some." She tilted a hand to indicate doubt.

"Want to?" I pushed my chair back from the table and stood.

"Sure." As Molly joined me, she added, "I was in a bowling league my freshman year, but I broke a finger the second week and had to quit."

"My freshman year I was the youngest kid playing varsity defense in the conference," The Bear observed in nostalgic tones.

"Spare me," said Megan.

The Bear poked a sturdy finger into her rib cage. "Be nice," he told her. "You are in the presence of a *star*."

Megan slapped at his finger, which Bear withdrew in a hurry. "Let's make a deal," she said. "You don't talk about football, and I won't talk about mousse and conditioners."

The Bear half closed his eyes as if he were thinking about it.

"No deal, no date," said Megan.

"Deal," agreed Bear. From the contented expression on his face, it was clear that at long last The Bear had found the perfect girlfriend.

21

*T*hat was several weeks ago. This Saturday, Molly and I are doubling with The Bear and Megan to the prom. Afterward we have reservations for dinner at The Elms, which is Bear's favorite restaurant.

Although it isn't official yet, it looks as if Benton is going to plead guilty to a charge of assault with a deadly weapon, plus poaching and shooting at federally protected wildlife. Lou told me this means that Benton will be able to fish, but it'll be a long time before he has a permit to hunt again. "And when he does," Lou added cheerfully, "no way will Benton find anyone to go with him. Hunters hate poachers."

"Do you have heart problems?" I asked Mrs. Burr this afternoon as I slid into my seat in front of her desk.

"Not that I know of." She peered at me over her half glasses. "Why?"

"Tomorrow's test on *Macbeth*," I told her. "My grade will be the biggest shock of the year."

"I'll try to remain calm." She looked toward the doorway, frowned, and moved from behind her desk back to the aisle.

Walking very slowly, Molly entered the room. Behind her, one hand on her shoulder and the other stretched tentatively before him, was Randall. Georgette followed Randall, carrying both their books.

Randall looked perfectly normal except for the red bandanna tied over his eyes.

"Now what?" asked Mrs. Burr.

"Psychology," explained Molly. "The students are finding out what it's like to be blind."

"Not in my class, they aren't."

"*Please*, Mrs. Burr," said Randall. "Mr. Wert's already depressed over how I messed up my marriage. If I foul this up, nobody'll get a decent grade for the semester."

"How long does this experiment last?"

"Just today."

"All right." As she stepped aside to let Molly and Randall pass, Mrs. Burr told the rest of us, "Open your books to page two-twenty-six, Act Five."

"Hold it!" said Randall. "I can't read my part!"

"I'll substitute for you," said Mrs. Burr.

"But it's my big death scene!"

"I'm sorry, Randall, but I can't cancel English class because of a psychology experiment." Mrs. Burr scanned the room. "Remember, Macbeth believes he's invincible. Not only will he defeat any man born of woman, but the three witches prophesied he would not die until Birnam Wood moved to Dunsinane."

I turned to Act Five. At this point in the play, Banquo's dead. As a matter of fact, most of the main characters have been slaughtered, but good old Macbeth is busily hacking away at the ones who remain.

We finished the scene where Malcolm ordered his soldiers to cut branches from the trees of Birnam Wood for camouflage. Back at the castle, Macbeth was organizing his forces when he heard a cry.

"Wherefore was that cry?" asked Macbeth.

"The queen, my lord, is dead," read JoJo, as Seyton.

"She should have died—"

"As winners of the candy sale, all seniors will now report to the auditorium for a movie."

There was stunned silence in our room, then scattered protests.

"Go on," Georgette urged Mrs. Burr.

Someone in the back row made a negative sound.

Mrs. Burr shook her head. She gestured toward the door with one hand, the other holding the place in her book.

Andy Howell stood and left, then Ty, Jerrilyn, and a group of girls.

"I'm staying," Georgette announced.

Mrs. Burr glanced at me, a tentative smile forming on her lips.

"No reason for me to leave," said Randall. "I couldn't see the stupid movie anyway."

Molly paused at the front of the room. "I was in charge of the candy sale," she told Mrs. Burr, "so I have to introduce the movie. After that, I'll be back."

When JoJo, his shoulders hunched, edged past her, Molly followed him out of the room. In the hall, she turned to blow me a kiss.

There were six students left in class, including me. I looked up at Mrs. Burr as she resumed Macbeth's part. Her eyes were brilliant behind her half glasses, the curve of her cheek round, her rusty gray hair caught back from her face by a green ribbon.

". . . Out, out, brief candle!" she read. "Life's but a walking shadow . . ."

22

After school, Molly and I drove out to the reservoir. In spite of a cold, gray rain, there were two other cars in the parking area. A man fishing from a rowboat probably owned one of the cars, but there was no sign of the other driver. I parked away from them, next to the woods.

Since rain was hitting my side of the car, I asked Molly to roll down her window. "So the windshield doesn't steam over," I explained. I moved closer to her. Except for the man in the rowboat, far out on the reservoir, we were alone. I put my arm around her, my hand moving on her shoulder, feeling the warmth of her hair.

"Look, Huey." Molly sat forward.

A weird-looking creature had appeared along the edge of the water. The bird was about the size of a crow, but walked in a crouch, its short orange legs bent and its long black bill pointed forward. The sides of the bird's head and neck were deep, rusty chestnut; its back, greenish black. Down the front of the neck and body ran white feathers striped with brown.

When the heron noticed the car, the black crest on top of its head slowly erected. Then the neck began to stretch, longer and longer, until it was equal to the length of the bird's body. Molly and I were closely regarded by one orange eye.

I held my breath.

The bird jerked, then stretched toward the water, distracted from us by the promise of a fish.

"What *is* it?" Molly whispered.

"Some kind of heron," I told her. I leaned over, my head close to hers, touching hers, as we watched the heron come closer, pass beyond the front of the car, and disappear behind the trees, out of sight.

ABOUT THE AUTHOR

A former high school English teacher, NANCY J. HOPPER began writing professionally while raising her two children. Since 1979, she has written eleven books for children and young adults, including *Wake Me When the Band Starts Playing*.

Of this book she notes, "I have been avidly interested in birds, their actions and habitats for most of my adult years. I believe (like Huey B!) that creatures like herons are not 'small stuff.' "

Mrs. Hopper lives in Alliance, Ohio, with her husband, a college art professor.